STAN E. HUGHES AKA HA-GUE-A-DEES-SAS

Mrs. Betts' Backyard

novum ◢ pro

This book is also
available as
e-book.

www.novumpublishing.com

© 2021 novum publishing

ISBN 978-1-64268-205-2
Cover photos: Evgenii Naumov, SaveJungle,
Punnawich Limparungpatanakij,
Taras Adamovych | Dreamstime.com
Cover design, layout & typesetting:
novum publishing

www.novumpublishing.com

Contents

CHAPTER 1

Penguins in the Backyard

Mrs. Betts lived in a normal 4-bedroom house across the street from a normal middle school in a normal neighborhood of a normal Pacific Northwest town.

(Editor's note: Too many 'normals'. Start over.)

(Sorry ...)

Mrs. Betts lived in a pleasant 4-bedroom house across the street from a busy middle school in a quiet neighborhood of a friendly Pacific Northwest town.

She was especially proud of her backyard with its variety of green trees, healthy bushes and many lovely flowers. She spent hours planting, watering and weeding until it was the showplace of the neighborhood. Stanley mowed the lawn once a week and keep the dandelions down, squirted Roundup weed killer on the weeds along the curb and in the driveway, and did most of the 'heavy work' to add to the pleasant feel of the yard. The wooden fence around the property provided just enough privacy without making the people next door feel like they weren't welcomed. Her hard work became quite famous among the nearby flower people and the local garden club was scheduled to drop by later in the week to determine if she would be the winner of the next Garden of the Month Award. Mrs. Ethel Mertz, garden club president, had contacted Mrs. Betts and they both couldn't wait to get together. Mrs. Betts loved to sit out on the patio under the sun umbrella with a fresh cup of coffee and think about ways to make her yard even nicer. Any new ideas from the garden club would be very welcomed.

Early one spring morning Mrs. Betts was awakened by a strange twittering-like clucking sound coming from her back yard. As she peered out the upstairs bedroom window, she could not believe her eyes: It was a small waddle of penguins!

(Editor's note: To hear what a waddle of penguins sounds like go to "google" and ask "What does a group of penguins sound like?")

"Stanley!" she shouted. "Wake up! There's a waddle of penguins in our backyard."

Stanley slowly sat up wiped his sleepy eyes and responded, "What's a waddle?"

Mrs. Betts could not believe his reaction. "That's what you are wondering about: What's a waddle? There are penguins in our backyard!"

Still in their 'jammies' they pulled on their slippers and hurried down the hall, across the dining room and out the back slider to see the sight more clearly. Sure enough, there was about a half dozen penguins happily wandering around the backyard eating flower blossoms and 'gakkering' to each other.

(Editor's note: "gakkering" is the scientific term for penguins having conversations with each other.)

The gate was still locked, there were no holes in the fence, and everyone knows penguins can't fly, so it was a real mystery how they got there.

Mrs. Betts collected herself and rambled on, "Well, they must belong to somebody. We should probably put a 'found six penguins' in the Lost and Found ads in the newspaper, let You-Tube and Facebook know what is going on, and maybe look on Craig's List for someone who was trying to sell them. Anyway, we should probably try to make them feel 'at home' while they are staying with us. Stanley, you run down to Wal-Mart and get one of those kids' plastic wading pools … No wait! You should probably get two of them. We'll fill them with water. I'll drive over to Egger's Meat Market and pick up some fresh fish. I think that is what they eat … Then maybe they will stop eating my flowers. Stanley, hurry along! This is kind of an emergency."

Next door, Officer Krupke, the neighborhood policeman, was looking over the fence with the same sense of wonder at what all the commotion was about. He took a deep drink of his coffee and commented, "Mrs. Betts, I don't know how those penguins got into you backyard, but you probably should take them to the zoo."

The next morning their neighbor woke up to that strange twittering-like clucking sound. He was kind of upset and growled, "Mrs. Betts, I told you to take those penguins to the zoo."

"I did," she answered. "We had so much fun, today we are going to the circus."

CHAPTER 2

Eureka! We Struck Oil!

Anyway, the trip to the circus with her penguins went okay. The circus owner felt the birds were so cute that he offered to take them along as part of the show. He promised to treat them nicely and give them lots of canned sardines, so Mrs. Betts thought that was probably best for them. She followed the circus's travels on the internet and her penguins were very popular wherever they traveled. The owner tied little red ribbons in the girl penguins' ears and had aviator caps made for the boys. The circus owner called them: "Mrs. Betts' babies."

Later in the summer, even though Mrs. Betts did win the Garden of the Month Award, she thought the backyard would be even nicer if they had a koi pond. This didn't interest Stanley very much because it sounded like a lot of hard work just to see a few big gold fish swimming around. There were plenty of cats in the neighborhood that would like nothing better than to climb over the fence, sneak into the backyard during the nighttime and try to catch a midnight snack.

But the more Mrs. Betts thought about how a koi pond would improve the appearance of her backyard the more convinced she was to make it happen.

Stanley argued, "But before you dig anyplace in the yard you have to call the power company on 811 and find out if it would be okay. They know where all the underground wires and cable television lines are buried, not to mention the natural gas pipes. They would be more than angry with us if we cut into something and inconvenienced everyone in the neighborhood."

"Don't be silly," Mrs. Betts retorted. "You can see that all the wires around here are on poles. There's nothing to worry about."

(Editor's note: In all the history of the world, the term "There's nothing to worry about" has probably caused more trouble than any earthquake or hurricane that has ever happened.)

So the work was about to begin.

Mrs. Betts decided the koi pond should be located in the middle of a large group of ferns and flowers in the center section of the yard where a couple of large ponderosa pine trees grew. There were two old concrete bird baths that Stanley always forgot to put water in nestled among the foliage. It didn't take the neighborhood birds long to realize it was a waste of time to try and stop by for a drink or short splash. In her mind Mrs. Betts could picture a small cool pleasant pond surrounded by lava rocks with large gold fish frolicking in the water. She was looking forward to feeding them and seeing them rise up to the surface to say '"thank you" before they enjoyed the treats. She unrolled a long strand of twine to outline the pond so Stanley would know where to start digging and thought a hole about three feet deep would work.

Not with the best of attitude, Stanley got the wheelbarrow, his shovel and pick-ax in preparation for the job waiting for him. He wasn't sure where to put the dirt he would dig, but Mrs. Betts said to dump it on the concrete pad next to the house where they used to store the Airstream Trailer and they could haul it away sometime later.

(Editor's note: The Airstream Trailer incident was still a sore point with Mrs. Betts and she would occasionally remind Stanley about it. One summer while on vacation Stanley had not properly connected the trailer to his truck and while crossing the bridge over the Grand Canyon in Arizona the trailer broke free, wobbled down the road a hundred yards or so, tumbled over the guard rail and plummeted a couple hundred feet into the Colorado River ... never to be seen again.)

It was summer time and the hot sun made the job even more unpleasant. Stanley could not believe how many big rocks were hidden in the dirt. Of course, it couldn't have been soft sand ... that would have been too easy. It was as much rocks and gravel as soil. Then he came across some giant roots from the pine trees which made it even more difficult. Digging down through three feet of what was waiting for him seemed almost impossible. He would chop – chop – chop with the pick-ax then shovel out the dirt and rocks and pieces of tree root into the wheelbarrow, roll the wheelbarrow around the house to the concrete pad, dump the wheelbarrow and then roll the wheelbarrow back to the work site to dig some more.

(Editor's note: Too many wheelbarrows. Rewrite this paragraph.)

(Okay. I don't know how many ways to say 'wheelbarrow' but I will try.)

… He would chop-chop-chop with the pick-ax then shovel out the dirt and rocks and pieces of tree root into the wheelbarrow, roll the conveyance around the house to the concrete pad, dump its contents and return to the work site to dig some more.

(Okay?)

(Editor's note: I'm not so sure it is 'better' but I'll take it.)

Mrs. Betts was enjoying watching Stanley dig her koi pond as she rested in a comfortable lawn chair on the patio under the sun umbrella putting new polish on her fingernails. A loud "clank" rolled out of the koi pond hole as Stanley was digging. Most of the digging sounds were "thunk", "clunk" or "crack" so a "clank" was very strange. Much to both of their amazements a thick black liquid began to exude from the small hole he had opened. He touched it with his fingers, took a closer look, and exclaimed, "Oh, my gosh! We've struck oil! We are going to be rich!"

Mrs. Betts was happy beyond belief! She yelled to Stanley, "You find the phone number for the Exxon Oil Company and tell them we have some oil to sell while I open up Amazon.com and start a list of things I want to buy! This is going to be 'the berries'. I'm going to order a swimming pool, a motorcycle, maybe a giraffe …"

(Editor's note: "The berries" is what old people used to say if something was great. Also this is one of those stories where everything does not necessarily go as planned. And this situation would be one of the first examples.)

As Mrs. Betts and Stanley were happily surfing the web for things to buy with their new found wealth a big white Toyota Tundra pickup with huge knobby tires rolled into the driveway. Two large men in blue jean coveralls with orange patches on the chests, bright yellow construction helmets, and long black beards climbed out. One was holding a clip board and neither was smiling. As they shut the truck doors the foreboding words painted on them was clearly evident: "Keystone Pipeline LLC – We bring oil to a thirsty nation."

"Are you Mrs. Betts," one of the men inquired as the front door was opened.

"Of course," she answered.

"Here's a bill for one thousand dollars. You poked a hole in the Keystone Pipeline and we have to repair it. Our equipment will be here in the morning. Oh, and I am apologizing ahead of time for the damage our trucks will do to your backyard …"

CHAPTER 3

Cats, Cats and more Cats

There were always cats around Mrs. Betts' backyard. Some people like dogs, a few people like frogs, but Mrs. Betts loved cats. Over the years she welcomed so many cats in her home that one of her friends gave her a coffee cup that said "One cat short of being a crazy cat lady." She invented a code to let Stanley know she couldn't answer the phone or that she needed a refill for her coffee cup and couldn't get up and get it. The code was "C.O.L" which means "Cat on Lap." She would never even dream of bothering a cat snoozing on her lap, so "C.O.L." became part of the daily conversation. Sometimes Stanley wanted "C.O.L." to mean "Cat over the Ledge", but he never said it out loud.

"Lucky the Cat" came into the family when Stanley found him one February in a casino parking lot. Or should we say Lucky the Cat found Stanley. The poor guy was basically fur and bones and seemed fearful as it hid under his truck. Obviously, scrounging for a living was not working very well. Stanley called Mrs. Betts and reported, "I'm bringing a guest home." Mrs. Betts' response of, "Okay. Who is it?" was answered simply, "A cat."

Lucky the Cat was totally black with just a few white hairs under his chin. As Stanley drove home with his new friend, it purred louder than the truck's engine and told him about the hard life he had endured by meowing constantly and looking for sympathy and pressing his head against Stanley's driving hand. Mrs. Betts' concerns about the health of this new family member were alleviated when their daughter came over to the house to check him out: Eyes clear, no mites in his ears, his claws and teeth seemed strong and his fur was as shiny as silk. Holding him in her lap she said, "This cat is so thin you can easily feel his ribs under his fur. It's going to take a while for him to fatten up." ... which he eventually did.

One problem: When Mrs. Betts would walk down the stairs from the bedroom with her sox on Lucky would attack her feet probably thinking they were something to play with. After a while her ankles looked like she had walked through a blackberry patch. Resolution: Off to the vet to remove his front claws, and while at it, take care of the other end. His recovery was brief and he became one of the friendliest and most engaging cats to ever live in the Betts' household. He was always there to greet visitors and make them feel at home. Even visitors who didn't necessarily like cats thought Lucky was kind of cool.

Lucky must have thought he was a miniature panther as he would creep through the flowers and ferns in the backyard pretending to be hunting some imaginary prey. He relished the attention of being the only animal on the property and this was justly deserved after the hard life he had lived before. Wouldn't you know it? Things were going too well ...

Enter Crabby "Natasha."

This old momma cat, was a different story. Mrs. Betts' daughter earned a great job on the east coast, so Natasha came to live with her new family. Obviously before she moved in she had been the queen of the house and she did not appreciate sharing her realm with anybody. Natasha didn't like Lucky ... at all ... from the very first day she arrived, and as time went by things never did improve. If Lucky was even in the room with her the old lady cat would hiss and growl at him, maybe take a couple swings at him, then dart under the bed until he was gone. More than one night Mrs. Betts and Stanley would be awaken by a cat fight. Mrs. Betts would yell, "You two go to your rooms until you can behave!" And usually things would quiet down. Like a lot of human people, as Natasha got older she began to lose her hair and it could be found clumped on the carpet or she would cough up a hair ball. Mrs. Betts was sure that under all that long frizzy hair was a precious hairless cat breed called 'the Sphynx' waiting to emerge. Sphynx cats are rare and very expensive, so everyone was hoping this would come to pass. As of this writing, the issue has yet to resolve itself.

Then along came "Tank." He was a Cornish Rex with white hair as soft as a rabbit's fur. Sometimes you really couldn't call him a 'white cat' because he loved to roll around on the concrete driveway and when he came in the house he was more 'light gray.' He might be best described as 'bulky' or just plain 'fat.' Mrs. Betts would say, "He wasn't fat ... he was fluffy." Tank loved the outdoors and would be happiest staying out all night having all kinds of adventures until the weather turned cold. Frankly, nobody knows what most cats do when they stay out all night so it is safe to assume it would be adventurous in some fashion. By morning he would be waiting at the front door to hit the cat food dish then find a nice chair to snooze away the day. On occasion Lucky would join him for his night prowl, and there would be two cats waiting at the front door in the morning. It was always a competition among family members to see what lap Tank would climb onto to meet the 'C.O.L' criteria. His soft fur and gentle nature made him very popular with everyone. Lucky seemed to accept him as a brother to team up against Natasha ... which of course, didn't set very well with the old momma cat so she would save a couple hisses, growls, and swipes for Tank.

The story of "Tigger' illustrates that not all cat stories are nice stories. When Tigger came to the Betts' home the aggressive feline decided that the other three cats were expendable. He was much larger and more muscular than the others so he would often try to bully them by chasing them under the sofa or by pushing them away from the food dishes. Since he thought he was too good to use the litter box the other cats used, he would relieve himself whenever and wherever he felt like it as much inside as outside. Finally, Mrs. Betts decided she had to draw the line and told Stanley to take Tigger to the humane society. One of the neighbor kids especially liked Tigger and would drop by to play with him now and then. When she saw Stanley drive away with him in the cat carrier she inquired what was going on and Mrs. Betts explained the situation. The little girl started crying and exclaimed, "That's where they kill animals! How could you do such an awful thing?" And she ran home in tears to tell on Mrs. Betts to her mom.

Mrs. Betts began to feel guilty about her plan and thought maybe she had been a little rash about her actions. She could get Tigger his own litter box and make sure he had his own food dish. Maybe she could train him into being more friendly and likeable. A trip to the vet with a couple of 'snip' 'snips' might bring that about if you know what that means. When Stanley returned from the humane society, she stated simply, "Go back and get the cat."

It wasn't that easy. Stanley returned to the humane society and said, "I guess I need to pick up the cat I just brought in."

The attendant replied, "Okay. Your cat is still in the waiting cage. However, it is company policy that all animals released into the community must be neutered, and he will need a rabies shot. Forty dollars, please. For another ten we will put a 'chip' in his neck so if he gets lost we can identify him …"

Stanley was not happy as he pulled two twenty dollar bills out of his wallet. He muttered, "Forget the chip. I hope he does get lost."

CHAPTER 4

Invasion of the Crows!

For some reason Stanley always liked crows. He could never quite explain why. He had traveled all over the United States in all kinds of weather conditions and always saw crows hanging around. They seemed comical, busy and sociable and possibly even enjoying life.

When he found out that a flock of crows is called "a murder." He just could not believe it. In his entire life he had never heard of such a weird thing, so he decided to call a flock of crows "caw-kers" since the noise crows make sounds like "caws"

(Editor's note: To hear the sounds crows make ask 'google' "What do crows sound like?" Clearly they are not song birds.)

Mrs. Betts decided it would be nice to put a bird bath in the flower beds in the front yard so she and Stanley drove over to the Home Depot garden shop and found a sturdy metal one that seemed to be just right. "We need to invite more song birds to come around. I think they would enjoy a chance to get a drink and maybe clean their feathers." She commented, then looked askance at Stanley, "For some reason I can't get my bird bath monitor to keep the bird baths in the back yard filled. Maybe if we have one in the front yard he will notice it more often."

The new bird bath was placed among the beautiful flowers and made a nice addition to the appearance of the front garden. As soon as Stanley filled it, strangely the neighborhood squirrels showed up and they happily jumped into the water taking refreshing drinks and having a great time. This was not exactly what Mrs. Betts had in mind, but it was okay.

Stanley watched them and decided, "If the squirrels are moving in I might as well put some squirrel food around the bird baths for them." A quick trip to the Pet Smart store resulted in a large bag of unsalted peanuts in the shell. He dumped a small pile on the ground and almost immediately after he stepped away the squirrels went for them. They would pick up a peanut in their little paws and eat it on the spot and spit out the shells. Now and then they would run off with one in their mouths and bury it in the flower bed.

(Editor's note: Well, this is a nice story. But what does that have to do with crows?)

(Just be patient! I'm getting to the point.)

A neighborhood crow was flying over the Betts' yard and noticed the new bird bath in the front garden. He (or she – it's impossible to decide if a crow is a boy or girl) soared down, perched on the edge of the bird bath and slurped up some of the nice cool water. The squirrels scattered not sure what would happen next. That was when the crow noticed what was left of the peanuts sprinkled on the ground. He dropped down, picked one up in his beak … and swallowed it whole! Then he ate a second and a third one. Stanley happened to be watching the squirrels at the time and was amazed at the crow's eating habits. "Well," he thought. "If the crows like the peanuts I better buy some more."

Big mistake!

It has never been proven, but scientists think that crows have a special ability to communicate with each other … even over long distances. It wasn't long before more and more crows began to soar around and perch in the tree limbs and on the bird bath cawing obnoxiously and dropping crow poop all over everything. Stanley would study them with his binoculars to see if he could tell one from the other. For two of them this was very easy. One was missing a leg, but he could perch on the bird bath and hop around on the ground with the rest of them. Stanley decided to call him "Huey." The other had something wrong with its left eye, so it was closed all the time. Stanley thought "Dewey" would be a good name for him. Try as he might, he could not distinguished another from the entire group that he hoped to call "Louie." So he named all the other crows hanging around: "Louie."

(Editor's Note: For those of you who don't live in the United States, "Huey" "Louie" and "Dewey" are Donald Ducks' nephews.)

The competition for the peanuts with the squirrels got pretty heated at times. A crow would fly down on the ground and a squirrel would charge at him before he had a chance to get the peanut so it would squawk and flap its wings in hopes of chasing away the squirrel. If a squirrel would grab a peanut and run off a crow or two would swoop down at him scaring him into dropping it in the front yard. It didn't take long for the combatants to eat every peanut Stanley had bought and that meant another trip to the Pet Smart store.

It started to be a real problem for the Betts family. If Stanley didn't keep the peanut supply up to date, the crows would sit in the tree limbs making quite a racket basically saying, "Stanley! Get with it! We want more peanuts! What's the matter with you?" Sometimes the racket would start early in the morning waking up the neighbors who began to get very grumpy. The squirrels would scurry around the front steps of the house or climb up on the window sills making a chattering sound which was their way of repeating exactly what the crows were saying to Stanley.

It got even worse. Mrs. Malone next door had a nice swimming pool in her back yard. She began to notice peanut shells and crow poop floating in the water and got very tired of scooping them up with a pool net. "This has got to stop!" she growled to Mr. Malone.

Later one morning a ring of the doorbell brought Stanley eye to eye with Mrs. Malone, Officer Krupke, and the Batemans who lived across the back fence. "Stanley," they said in agreement. "You have got to do something about all those crows. They are a nuisance and we will have to report you to the authorities if you don't take care of the problem."

Stanley poo-pooed their concern, "I didn't know there was a crow police force in this town."

Officer Krupke stepped forward and said menacingly, "I do have my Red Ryder b-b gun, Stanley. If you don't deal with the crows. I will."

The neighbors walked back down the front steps looking back clearly not satisfied with the confrontation.

Mrs. Betts walked up and stood beside Stanley at the front door, "Well, Mr. Conservation, what's your plan? We have to get along with our neighbors. I think you know that."

Stanley was resigned to the situation. "You're right. I will figure out something. I really enjoyed having all the crows around and watching them and the squirrels chasing each other."

After Stanley stopped putting peanuts out, it didn't take long for both the squirrels and crows to realize their meal ticket had expired. The crows stopped hanging around begging for treats and the squirrels returned to their nests getting them ready for winter. Sometime later Mrs. Malone brought over a pan of homemade biscuits to thank the Betts for dealing with the issue at hand and Officer Krupke became less threatening. They never did hear from the Batemans across the back fence but that wasn't anything new. The Batemans pretty much never talked to anybody.

CHAPTER 5

Born on the 4ᵗʰ of July? ... Nah

The 4th of July was always a very festive and colorful holiday at the Betts' household. Stanley was a veteran of the U.S. Army and many of Mrs. Betts' friends and family had served their country over the years. In her mind, this was a unique and important opportunity to say "Thank you for your service."

Mrs. Betts worked diligently on the menu for her famous bar-b-que as Stanley began inviting people with the many phone calls needed. Nobody ever said "no." Mrs. Betts' kitchen was famous almost from coast to coast and her homemade potato salad was featured on "The Ellen DeGeneres Show." An invitation from the Betts' household was a very, very special honor and deeply coveted by the recipients.

While Mrs. Betts developed the items for the menu, Stanley also had an important responsibility:

The fireworks!

At least a month before the party he would begin researching on the computer which are the best fireworks and where to find them. Once he had the needed information and made his shopping list he would drive over to the nearby Indian Reservation and place his order. The fireworks salespeople were always happy to see his pickup truck roll into the parking lot and eager to help him in any way possible. Stanley had a mathematical formula for determining how many fireworks to buy:

Number of guests – subtract number not interested in participating – times how much money he had to spend.

When he got to the fireworks stand on the reservation, he went a little 'nuts', completely forgot his formula, and bought everything he wanted: Fountains, sparklers, rockets, all kinds and sizes of firecrackers, bottle rockets, cones, helicopters, Roman candles, and jumping jacks. Lucky for him he drove his pickup truck or he would have had to order a couple Ubers.

Stanley always wanted to buy some of those big fireworks rockets that you see on television or at big 4th of July displays in the city or at the ball park. However, they were not for sale for individual people. I guess there were just too many regulations and too many chances for serious accidents. So … not to be dissuaded, he decided to build his own and use it as the finale for his neighborhood fireworks show. The fireworks stand on the reservation was able to sell him three of the smaller rockets, each about two feet long, and his mind ran wild as he planned to turn them into a three-stage rocket. This was going to be "the berries."

When he got home he unloaded his fireworks treasures in the garage then hurried directly to his 'man cave' downstairs in hopes that Mrs. Betts would not see what he was up to. She was so busy preparing all the treats for the party she barely noticed him. "Stanley," she called. "I have a list of items I need from the grocery store. Can you picked them up for me?"

"Of course," he answered in a friendly fashion. "I have a small project to work on, then I would be happy to go."

He laid the three rockets on his work table and had two problems to solve: How to connect them together and how to get each one to ignite in the proper order. Joining them together into one big rocket was easy: Duck-tape. Then he realized he had lots of firecrackers that he could remove the fuses from then attach them to each other to make a long string of fuses to carry the fire from one rocket to the next. Perfect! He felt a strong sense of satisfaction as he assembled his marvelous three-stage rocket. For a finishing touch he spray-painted it a glistening gold color. It was his plan to launch it in the school yard across the street, and since it would be dark by the time everyone had set off all the normal fireworks it would be a surprise for everyone. Cool!

What a glorious celebration that evening! Mrs. Betts had outdone herself preparing the menu and everyone crowded around the tables set up on the back patio eating and visiting. Friends and neighbors reconnected after not seeing each other since the prior 4th of July, so they had plenty to visit about. They all knew the big 'bang' would be setting off the fireworks in the driveway after it started to get dark and they were eager to either participate or watch. As the evening moved forward Stanley directed them to get their chairs and come around to the front of the house. He opened the garage and a glorious display of fireworks were at the ready for everyone to enjoy. Which they did in great gusto!

Later when it had started to get totally dark Stanley had stepped away from the party and quietly carried his three-stage rocket and a square of plywood to set up on the school yard. As the last of the regular fireworks were set off, he asked everyone to stay put and be ready for a marvelous event. He disappeared into the night, walked over to the waiting rocket in the school yard and lit the fuse of the first stage. It burst into a kaleidoscope of shocking colors of reds and yellows and growled menacingly as it slowly rose above the ground. Most rockets shoot up into the air in the blink of an eye, so clearly this was a problem. Maybe the two stages attached to the top of rocket-one were too heavy. Then like all those problems back in the early days of the United States trying to get into space … something went wrong! The first stage burst into an ear splitting explosion of fire and light, the two other stages toppled over and also caught on fire and sped parallel to the ground in a crazy wobbling trajectory. Everyone ducked or ran for cover fearful for their lives! As the vestiges of the rocket sped toward the school building an unsettling 'crash' let everyone know something bad had happened and they could hear the fire alarm at the school blaring out: "Warning! Warning!"

To this day some kind of record must have been set for a large party of people and their automobiles disappearing into the night. I have heard rumors that some kids' parties clear out in seconds when the parents come home. By the time the fire department arrived at the school the entire neighborhood was so quiet you could hear a pin drop. Fortunately, the rocket had pretty much expended itself by the time it hit the school so it broke a window but didn't burn the building down. Later a couple of investigators from the fire department knocked on the doors of nearby houses to find out if anybody knew anything. This was a tight and cordial neighborhood, so nobody 'ratted' on Stanley, and eventually the fire department decided the cause of the damage was: 'Unknown.'

CHAPTER 6

Isn't That Just Ducky?

(Editor's note: The incident in Chapter 2 when Mrs. Betts and Stanley thought they had struck oil did not end when the chapter ended. The purpose of the Keystone Pipeline was to transfer crude oil from the shale oil fields in Alberta, Canada, to waiting refineries in the United States. People were concerned about the damage to the environment because of construction of the pipeline and also possible oil spills after it was completed. Keystone Pipeline had developed an emergency response computer system to detect pressure losses in the line and to immediately shut down the flow of oil until it could be dealt with. Mrs. Betts and Stanley had rushed to their computer lap tops in the house to contact Exxon Oil and to look at items they wanted to buy, so they didn't realize that the oil seeping out of the hole almost immediately stopped, which basically saved the backyard. Had it kept running an entire backyard swimming in crude oil could not win any Garden of the Month awards.).

Mrs. Betts sat on the patio with tears in her eyes. The pipeline company had to bring in a machine called a 'back hoe' to dig around the oil spill in preparation for the needed repairs. They had to take down the gate that connected the west end of the house to the fence that separated her property from Mrs. Malone's. Then the heavy machine with giant tires had to roll across the backyard to the location of the problem leaving tread marks and tearing up some of the beautiful grass. The situation got worse when a large dump truck backed across the lawn to receive the dirt being dug out of the hole until it could be put back in the work site.

That's when Mrs. Betts had a brilliant idea. Because the back hoe was digging around the pipeline she wondered if she could talk the operator into making the hole large enough that she might still be able to have her koi pond. The worker thought a moment and responded, "Why not? Once I am done digging and the repair crew fixes the hole, we have to cover the surrounding ground with concrete so it won't be cut again. Let's give it a try."

Mrs. Betts ran into the kitchen to get her ball of twine and laid out the boundary for the koi pond. Since the machine was doing all the work and Stanley didn't have to dig by hand … she made the shape of the koi pond much, much larger. Before long the repair to the pipeline was completed. The hole Stanley punched was really not that big, so things went quickly. As the crew mixed up the concrete, Mrs. Betts called, "Stanley, come and see what's going on! I'm going to have my koi pond after all."

And she did.

After all the big equipment left, the pipeline company repaired the gate and even had someone from a local lawn service drop by and do some repairs on the damage to the yard. They decided to not charge the thousand dollars they had previously expected. They knew how popular Mrs. Betts was in the community and thought this good will gesture would be the best for everyone. Many people felt more positive about the Keystone Pipeline when they learned of this action.

It took a while for the concrete to set and by the time the koi pond was ready for Stanley to put water in it, the dimensions of the pond were fifteen feet long, ten feet wide and almost three feet deep. This was exactly what Mrs. Betts had hoped for, and she was as happy as a clam.

(Editor's note: This is a nice story and all, but what does that have to do with "Isn't That Just Ducky?")

(Keep reading, please).

Mrs. Betts and Stanley drove over to Northwest Seed and Pet to pick out some of the koi fish. She wanted two or three orange ones, a couple yellow ones, and maybe two or three that were beautifully spotted with colors as bright as the sun. She was also able to buy a supply of fish food and a book on how to raise and take care of koi fish. Stanley was quietly happy knowing she would be busy with her fish so he could watch more old movies on Turner Classic Movies with less interruptions.

Then she did something very unexpected: The store had just received a shipment of baby ducks. They were so cute quacking merrily and waddling around in the pen that she just had to have one. Stanley just shook his head as she picked out one that especially caught her eye. While the majority of the ducklings in the pen were yellow, this one seemed to be a little more toward the brown color. The store worker put him in a cardboard box and they weren't even home yet when she decided to name him "Ducky." Stanley wondered if she was also going to name all the koi fish but kept shut about it not wanting to give Mrs. Betts any more ideas.

Now the picture is almost complete. Stanley carefully placed the fish in the pond and released "Ducky" who started swimming around quacking in great joy. This was the first sense of freedom he had felt after spending most of his young life in that pen at the pet store … and it was exhilarating. Mrs. Betts found some lily pads in a nearby lake and replanted them in the koi pond. She then tidied up the grounds around the pond and added some beautiful flowers before calling the garden club and inviting them out to see how the backyard had changed. Stanley went over to Pool World and bought an aerator for water circulation and also came home with an assortment of tools to be used to keep the pond clean and fresh. He had planned to teach Mrs. Betts how to use the tools so he could 'wash his hands' of the whole situation.

Having "Ducky" in the backyard proved to be a pretty good idea. As he grew bigger his wings got stronger and his feathers were a thick gray color that seemed to glisten in the sunlight. He would explore around the property digging up worms and grubs in the soil and became aggressive enough to chase away neighbor dogs and any crows or herons who might have wanted to taste Mrs. Betts' koi fish. All the family cats learned early to stay away from "Ducky" so they had declared a truce instead of declared a duck versus cat war. When

Mrs. Betts and Stanley were sitting on the lawn chairs under the sun umbrella on the back deck he would waddle over, climb up on a chair, and just hang out as he were another member of the family … which clearly… he was.

Stanley had to admit he had grown rather fond of "Ducky." The friendly bird would watch what his people were eating and try to get a bite for himself. Normally, ducks eat the worms and insects they find but he was willing to try popcorn, apple slices, and other fruit and vegetables. If he didn't like it he would let out a loud 'quack' and spit it out. If he liked it, he would beg for more. Whenever Mrs. Betts and Stanley would be working in the garden the duck would follow them around as if he were a trained doggie and dig through the dirt piles looking for worms. One time Stanley put a leash around his neck and took him for a walk around the neighborhood. The duck did not fuss about it at all and wherever they went kids and adults would tag along taking pictures on their cell phones and asking how it came about. "Ducky" and Stanley were the hit of 23rd Avenue and tried to take walks together as much as possible. Mrs. Betts perused 'Google;' to try to determine what kind of duck their pet was. When she saw a picture of a Northern Pintail it was clear that was his heritage. How an egg from a wild duck found itself among eggs from normal white farm ducks was a mystery. Northern Pintails were migrating birds that could fly tor hours if they chose. "Ducky" never even tried to fly. His life was great just the way it was.

Most good stories have a sad part, and this one is no different. One late autumn day "Ducky" was foraging around the backyard when he heard a distant quacking noise. He looked up and saw a large v-formation of wild ducks migrating south for the winter. He didn't understand it, but he suddenly had a strong urge to join them. He looked at the backyard which was his home and thought about his people who he just adored, but he couldn't resist the Call of the Wild, flapped his wings and flew away to eagerly join the other ducks

Later, Stanley came down the stairs from the office and walked into the kitchen. "Have you seen 'Ducky'? He asked Mrs. Betts.

She thought a moment, then responded, "Now that I think about it I haven't seen him all day. I've been busy making homemade soup."

Stanley lifted the lid off the boiling soup pot and saw the legs, wings and neck of the poor creature being cooked. In total shock and dismay he looked at Mrs. Betts, "How could you? He was our pet!"

Mrs. Betts gave Stanley 'the look' and answered, "Don't be silly. I'm making chicken soup."

(Editor's note: Scientists have studied the flight patterns of migrating birds and have determined that the paths they take when flying south are basically the same ones they take when returning north. There is a good chance that Ducky will fly over the Betts' house in the spring, drop away from the 'v' formation and reunite with his people. He might even bring a friend along.)

CHAPTER 7

Food on the Table?

One early spring day Mrs. Betts was reading an article in the newspaper about "Food Gardening." This was a popular method of planting vegetables in and among the flowers in a garden. She looked over the flower beds all around the house, and clearly there was plenty of room to try this idea.

Stanley was watching an old movie on the Turner Classic Movies channel as Mrs. Betts walked into the living room. "Stanley," she inquired. "What are your favorite vegetables?"

He was somewhat annoyed by the interruption and growled, "I don't like any vegetables except baked potatoes. If God wanted me to eat vegetables he would have given me four legs and a tail."

Mrs. Betts accepted his reply as permission to go forward with her Food Gardening idea, so she sat down at the kitchen table and started a list of vegetables she liked: Carrots ... green beans ... snap peas ... beets ... different kinds of tomatoes ... corn ... sun flowers ... cucumbers ... squash ... pumpkins ... radishes ... onions ... basil ... rhubarb and zucchini. Then she crossed off zucchini because everyone grew them and handed them out all around the neighborhood.

One Halloween Mrs. Malone handed out small zucchinis to the kids who Trick or Treated her house. Needless to say, they were not very happy with the idea, and some of them came back later in the night and threw eggs at her front door. Mrs. Betts finally found a decent zucchini bread recipe so didn't mind when Mrs. Malone came over with a huge sack full.

Then she re-read the article in the paper to learn how to prepare the flower beds for vegetables. The article recommended mixing in 'potting soil' and some special 'fertilizers' so the ground would have enough nutrients to grow the vegetables as well as flowers. It also recommended about how much of each to spread around for maximum success. As she calculated her potential need … it was quite a few 30 pound bags from the Home Depot garden store. She knew Stanley would not be too happy having to lift all those bags and deposit them around the flower beds so she had a crafty idea. "Stanley, after your movie would you like to go down to Mike's for fresh donuts?"

"Of course!" he replied enthusiastically. "That's a great way to start the day!"

"If it's okay, could we make a quick stop at Home Depot on the way … and take the pickup truck?" she continued.

"No problem."

So much for the "quick stop" idea. By the time Mrs. Betts had purchased all the different kinds of vegetable seeds, tomato starts, and bags of soil and fertilizer they had the entire bed of the pickup filled to the gills. Stanley was not happy at all realizing he was the 'loader', 'unloader', and 'spreader' for the upcoming project. Mrs. Betts was so optimistic and excited about all the food they would harvest, he just bit his lip and kept his thoughts to himself. Over the years this method had saved him a lot of grief. Unfortunately, by the time they finished shopping and arrived at Mike's Donuts, he was closed for the day. Stanley just rolled his eyes and wished for a quick death.

(Editor's note: Someone once calculated how much a home grown vegetable actually costs if you included water, fertilizers and labor. It would have been cheaper by far to go to the grocery store.)

Due to many years of gardening Mrs. Betts knew the best way to plant things so it would maximize the sunlight and the use of water: Put the tall plants behind the middle size plants and then the short plants in front. She could picture in her mind how beautiful her garden would look with the vegetables in all their colorful glory glistening in the morning sunlight. She couldn't wait to pick the first snap pea or tomato off the vine and enjoy its fresh juicy flavor.

Stanley got his wheelbarrow, shovel, and rake and begrudgingly helped Mrs. Betts with the planting. After all the seeds were in the soil the watering and weeding started and it was time to wait … and to wait … and to wait.

(Editor's note: What's with all the "… and to waits …"? That's called 'redundancy' you know.)

Some problems started right away, when the squirrels saw Mrs. Betts put the sunflower seeds in the earth, they waited around until she went in the house, then rushed down and dug them all up, enjoying a few as they took the rest to their nest. She was not happy when she came out to check her work and got so mad she was going to build some kind of scare-crow to keep the squirrels at bay. Stanley said "scare-squirrels" have never worked so she gave up on that idea. Mrs. Betts was very pleased the way her rhubarb was growing and couldn't wait to bake her first strawberry-rhubarb pie. One morning while picking up the newspaper in the driveway, she looked at her rhubarb plant and noticed the leaves were frayed and full of holes. The slugs had discovered the delicious morsel and made quite a meal out of it. That brought about another trip to Home Depot for slug bait. Mrs. Betts loved all animals, so felt a little guilty setting up the trap to finish off the perpetrators.

When the first little plants started to poke their heads out of the soil, Mrs. Betts was more than happy. She had made a map of what was where so knew what was growing even though it wasn't possible to tell at this early stage. "Stanley!" she yelled. "Come and see the garden! The peas (or whatever) are starting."

I guess it was when the beets popped up that finally drove Stanley over the edge. In past years he had some bad experiences with beets. He must have been allergic to them because the way they would make his tummy ache after having some as part of a meal. He finally realized "no beets!" and that was the last time he ate them. He could not in clear conscience live with the fact that they were growing on his property. Early one morning when he was able to identify the growing beets and Mrs. Betts was still asleep, he quietly got his spray bottle of Roundup weed killer and blasted them to kingdom come.

To this day, Mrs. Betts could never figure out why all the vegetables grew so well year after year except for the beets.

CHAPTER 8

Stanley's Little Bother ... I Mean Brother

Mrs. Betts was enjoying her coffee and admiring her beautiful yard from the lawn chair on her front porch. She always liked to get up before Stanley and relax in the peace and quiet of an early summer morning. The birds were happily chirping and the squirrels were running across the grass trying to find some of the peanuts Stanley always had scattered in the flower beds for them.

As her eyes wandered toward the sidewalk she saw a disturbing sight. Parked against the curb and partly on the front grass was an old Volkswagen mini-van. It was so rusty and beat up that it was hard to determine its original color. The front bumper was missing and the "V" on the front of the bus had been dented so many times it looked more like a "W." One of the side windows was missing and had been replaced by a piece of plywood held in place by strips and strips of duct tape. The tires did not match each other in any way. A deep tread winter snow tire was on the front right wheel and a small oval 'donut' was on the right back wheel. The kind of tire you should only use while you are waiting for one of your regular tires to be repaired. All kinds of stickers had been attached on the doors with old sayings like "Get U.S. out of Vietnam" or "Honk if you like Jimmy Carter" or "Janice Joplin for President" and a whole bunch of stickers that just said "Peace."

Mrs. Betts hurried back into the house and straight to the bedroom. "Stanley! Get up! Homeless people are moving into our neighborhood!" Tell them to park some-place else!"

Stanley opened up one sleepy eye and responded, "Are they in a car or something? And are they on the street."

"I don't know what kind of car it is," Mrs. Betts answered. "It is such a mess nobody could figure it out. And yes, they are parked on the street right in front of the house."

Stanley rolled over and mumbled, "The streets are public property. Unless they start causing a problem, they have every right to be there. Good night."

Mrs. Betts returned to the front porch not really sure what to do next. Then a very strange thing happened. Someone opened up the driver side door of the mini-van. He had so much hair and his beard was so shaggy that he looked like a brown floor mop with eyes. He was wearing denim coveralls that looked like they desperately need some washing machine time and an old fashioned tie-dye T-shirt that had a faded peace sign on it. He walked around the back of the mini-van and said in a friendly manner, "Is Ted around? I'm his little brother Ol-ee-ver."

Editor's note: Stanley (also known as "Ted" or "Teddy") and his little brother Ol-ee-ver were orphans in San Diego, California. When they stepped onto the sidewalk of life they had many interesting and exciting adventures together. These were written-up in the New

York Times Bestseller and the Cadbury Award winning book "Grandpa's Childhood" available from Dork and Sons Publishers in Philadelphia.

Mrs. Betts just stood there with her mouth open. Stanley had never talked much about his childhood, so she wasn't sure what to believe. She just shook her head and went back into the house. "Stanley!" she called. "There's a man on the front yard who says he is your little brother Ol-ee-ver."

Stanley bolted out of bed, put on his slippers and rushed down the steps to the living room. "Did he say Ol-ee-ver? I can't believe it!"

Sure enough, it was his little brother. Stanley was so pleased to see him after so many years he bubbled forth, "Come in! We can have a cup of coffee and talk about old times! What have you been doing? We've got a lot of catching up to do."

Ol-ee-ver smiled then replied, "Do you mind if we sit on the porch? Whenever I am in a house it feels like someone is squeezing me. I am really more comfortable outdoors."

Stanley was in no condition to refuse his little brother. "Sounds good to me. Sit down and tell me everything."

Mrs. Betts brought out a couple cups of fresh coffee and joined them on the porch. Ol-ee-ver sat back in the lawn chair, closed his eyes for a moment, then began: "I think we really enjoyed living with Grandpa and Grandma on their farm. Later on you had gone off and joined the Army while I was still in school. I heard they had a hard time believing that you had already been in the service until they saw the tattoo on your arm from Subic Bay in the Philippines. I got a job at the pet store in town grooming cats." He held up his arms and they were covered with cat scratch scars from his wrists to his forearms. "Everyone knows cats don't like to take baths so they took their anger out on me. Ouch!"

At that moment the four cats living with Stanley and Mrs. Betts walked over to the screen door and looked at Ol-ee-ver. It seemed like they were admiring what their cousin cats had done to him.

Ol-ee-ver continued, "Grampa wanted me to stay on the farm and help him. I liked being outdoors and watching things grow, but I guess I was too restless after our years on the road together to stay around very long. I made enough money at the pet store to buy the Volkswagen mini-van that Mr. McDonald down the road had in his back yard for who knows how long. Grampa and I towed it back to our place and I worked on it to see if I could get it going again. When I realized it was ready for the big start-up I asked Grampa and Grandma to come out and watch me fire it up. I turned on the key and pushed the starter button and there was a loud 'bang' and a huge cloud of smoke shot out of the tail pipe. I think I killed every mosquito on the property. Then it started to run and pretty soon it sounded like a purring kitten."

"I knew you were stationed with the Army in Boston, Massachusetts, so I decided to work my way across the country and try to get there about the time you were ready to be discharged. Then I would try to talk you into traveling with me like in the old days."

"My next job was at a large turkey farm in southern Idaho. My responsibility was "feather plucker." We had a long assembly line of dead turkeys. I would drop one into a big vat of hot water, slosh it around for a few minutes, then the feathers could be picked off easily. We would put the feathers in a big metal trailer, then when it was full take them out to the dump and have them burned. I thought that was very wasteful, so I collected up a bunch of feathers, dyed them different colors and sewed them onto strips of cloth to make Indian headdresses. I gave them to the kids in town and pretty soon every kid would come by on their bicycles with their colorful headdresses blowing in the breeze. My boss saw this a way to make some extra money, so he took all the feathers and put them in big vats of different colored dyes. He would have us lay them out on this concrete floor to dry then load them up in giant clear plastic bags. He sold the feathers to Mattel Toy Company and did okay for himself. He would let me park the mini-van on the property so I didn't have to pay anybody rent and pretty soon had a nice nest egg built up for the next leg of my trip."

Stanley and Mrs. Betts were getting into Ol-ee-ver's story and were eager to hear more.

"While driving across Iowa I went by a dairy farm that had a 'help wanted' sign in their front yard. When they found out I had grown up on Grandpa and Grandma's farm they put me to work right away. The dairy was so big and had so many cows it was almost organized like a factory. I had an official job title: Apprentice Poop Scooper. You guessed it. My job was to take a shovel and a wheelbarrow and go around scooping cow poop. When I had loaded up the wheelbarrow I would push it over to a large sink hole at the corner of the property and dump my load. There was a pile of wood chips next to the sink hole so I would throw a couple shovelfuls on top of the poop and go back to the dairy. Sometimes the boss would have two or three of us go out to the pasture to do some scooping. The piles there had dried in the sun so they weren't gross at all. The other guys called them "cow pies." They kind of looked like light brown Frizbies. I picked one up and tossed it toward my wheelbarrow and it took off just like a Frizbie! I showed the other guys what had happened and pretty soon we were throwing 'cow pies' all over the place. It was really fun. I found out later that sailing 'cow pies' became really popular around there and they actually had a 'cow pie' sailing contest every year that people came from miles around to participate in. You know? I never got credit for that idea."

Stanley interrupted the story. "I don't want you to stop, but let's make you feel more at home. We have a very comfortable guest bedroom with its own shower and bathroom. We'll set you up in there and I have lots of extra clothes to share with you if you need them."

Ol-ee-ver seemed surprised. "Did you say "shower'? I don't take showers they wash away my protective coating."

Mrs. Betts could only respond, "Protective coating?"

I have discovered," Ol-ee-ver continued, "That if a person doesn't take a shower the human body will eventually build up a protective coating on the skin that will keep him from getting sick, will ward off any mosquito bites, and will help keep him cool in the summer time. If it is okay with you I will just set up my tent in your back yard."

Stanley looked at Mrs. Betts and they decided there really wasn't any other choice at this moment. Later as they sat together on the back patio whey watched Ol-ee-ver set up his camp site. He had an old Army pup tent that he erected quickly and efficiently. Then he collected up some of the larger rocks around the yard and made a small fire circle. He had an old rusty hatchet and began chopping off dead branches from the nearby trees for his campfire. Once the fire was going okay, he took an iron frying pan out of his knapsack and placed it over the flames. Then he did something so shocking both Stanley and Mrs. Betts could not believe their eyes. He walked over to the koi pond, caught a medium sized gold fish in his hands and as it thrashed and wiggled he plopped it into the hot frying pan.

Mrs. Betts gasped, "That was Chloe! One of my favorites!"

Ol-ee-ver removed the fried fish from the pan with a fork and began eating it … guts and bones and all.

Mrs. Betts looked at Stanley and said sharply, "I don't care who he is. This is definitely not going to work."

Stanley had to agree.

Poor Stanley was really in a quandary. He and his little brother had been through so much together as homeless orphans on their own. Ol-ee-ver was the last living member of his family and even though they had not seen each other for a very long time they still had a special bond that only brothers know about. That night around his campfire, Stanley and Ol-ee-ver talked long into the night. It really was one of those longed dreamed of summer evenings when the sky is brilliant with stars and a gentle breeze brings that pleasant aroma of summer flowers.

Mrs. Betts watched them from the bedroom window and tried to determine if anything was about to be decided. As far as she was concerned Ol-ee-ver would be on his way in the morning.

Much later Stanley came to bed clearly on the horns of a dilemma. He did not want to lose track of his little brother after all these years, but he didn't want to get into an argument with his sweet heart.

Mrs. Betts looked kindly at her man then offered a suggestion that might be the best of both worlds. "Ol-ee-ver is definitely an outdoors man. Clearly he can survive in any conditions and he even seems to enjoy the challenge. I was thinking. We own 160 acres of forest land on the Indian reservation up by the Canadian border. We always worry that there might be a wild fire or that those people called 'survivalists' who claim to want to live "off the grid" and out of touch with society will sneak onto our land and try to live there. There is an old run-down cabin on the property that we had planned to make livable someday. Let's see if Ol-ee-ver would be willing to live up there for a while and keep an eye on the place for us. Maybe work on updating the cabin and thinning out some of the extra trees and underbrush that might help a fire. We could pay him for his time and you would be able to drive up and see him whenever you want.

The next morning Ol-ee-ver was already busy preparing for his next meal. Which would have been another koi fish if Stanley hadn't take out a plate of French toast and bacon. He sat down next to his brother and started the conversation. "What are your next plans?"

"I dunno," Ol-ee-ver answered. "I usually don't make any plans … just go with the flow."

"Would you be willing to help your big brother with a little problem?" Stanley asked.

Ol-ee-ver sat up and said, "Of course! You know I would do anything for you."

Stanley told him about Mrs. Betts' ideas for their property in the northeast corner of the state. "Well, I would have to take a look at it first." He responded.

So plans were made to take a trip to the area. Mrs. Betts packed a big lunch for the boys and a small suitcase of extra clothes in case they might need them. Stanley and Ol-ee-ver loaded up some tools and had a great time traveling together in Stanley's pickup truck and talked all the way there. As soon as Ol-ee-ver saw the property he had a feeling that he was finally 'home' and he couldn't wait to get started.

Over the next months or so Ol-ee-ver really spruced the place up and he was so handy with woodworking and tools that the cabin began to look pretty good. Stanley would keep in touch and bring any items Ol-ee-ver needed for his plans and both enjoyed each other's company. Stanley gave Ol-ee-ver a cell phone, but there wasn't any service so far out in the mountains. He would drive his old Volkswagen mini-van into the little town about 20 miles away where there was service and call Stanley whenever he needed to. While in town a friendly lady who worked in the only restaurant would let him charge up his phone if it needed to be. Later Stanley found out that Ol-ee-ver had made friends with the lady who worked at the restaurant and she really liked 'mountain men.' It was only a matter of time before Ol-ee-ver asked her if she would like to see his project. There was a rumor that she liked it so much she decided to move in. If this turns out to be true, we will let you know.

Don't ask me about his 'protective coating' idea. Just the thought of it still makes me uncomfortable.

CHAPTER 9

Hot Tub Mystery

You know that the nice weather is on the way when Mrs. Betts and Stanley bring up the patio furniture that had been stored all winter in the basement. The round glass table, extra-large sun umbrella with solar battery LED lights and folding chairs all take the assigned places they have enjoyed for countless summers. Then Mrs. Betts concocts her famous ginger ale and cranberry juice cocktails and they sit in comfort enjoying their beautiful backyard.

"You know what we need now?" Mrs. Betts inquired to Stanley. "We need a hot tub. Everyone in the neighborhood has one."

Stanley gave Mrs. Betts a sideways glance and said, "We have a koi pond. Don't you think that's enough water for anybody's backyard?"

Ignoring Stanley's less than enthusiastic response, Mrs. Betts continued, "Discount Spas is having a great sale on a 6-person octagon-shaped all electric model with three bubbler speeds. Doesn't it sound nice to have a stream of warm bubbles massaging your aching back?"

"What sounds nice to me is talking you into giving me a back rub while we watch 'Jeopardy' on our 65 inch TV," Stanley replied quietly under his breath, then he answered, "If we got a hot tub, where would we put it? There isn't much room left in our backyard even for more flowers."

"Nonsense," responded Mrs. Betts. "I have always wanted to extend the patio further toward Mrs. Malone's fence. All we need to do is put down a concrete slab to set the hot tub on, then build the patio around it and connect the new section to the rest of the patio. Piece of cake!"

"Piece of cake," thought Stanley. "More like a sore back, aching knees, and a trip to the chiropractor."

"My cousin Gregg is quite the handyman. I bet we could hire him to do all the work," Mrs. Betts rambled on. "I'll call him and see if he is available."

(Editor's note: Well, Cousin Gregg was available … and the rest is history.)

It was quite a sight for the neighbors as the project slowly came together. Mrs. Betts' cousin did a masterful job, the spa people brought out the hot tub and installed it. Then Cousin Gregg continued building the patio around the tub including a small fence for extra privacy. The finished product was a sight to behold. Mrs. Betts hosted a 'Welcome – Come and see our new hot tub" party and, of course, the whole neighborhood attended … adults, children and pets. Everyone wanted to try the hot tub but Mrs. Betts was careful to explain they would have to be put on a waiting list and take turns. This didn't exactly interest anyone since most had their own hot tubs anyway.

As the spring wandered into summer Mrs. Betts and Stanley really enjoyed the new addition to their backyard. They especially liked to soak out under the night skies and watch the twinkling stars. Responding to the oncoming hot weather, they decided to cool the tub down so it would almost be like a small swimming pool, and this worked great. When the grandkids found out about the plan they couldn't wait to visit and splash around in the tub. Stanley completed the finishing touches making sure the water was fresh and clean and at a comfortable temperature ... not too hot or not too cold.

As he surveyed the situation, he suddenly had a brilliant idea: If he went over to the Northwest Seed and Pet Store he could buy some little gold fish and the children would have a wonderful time swimming around with them. In no way did he want the kids wading around in the koi pond, so this would be an acceptable alternative. He shared his idea with Mrs. Betts, but she wasn't overly supportive about the plan. She couldn't think of anyone who had ever thought about putting gold fish in a cooled down hot tub. She could picture a thousand reasons why it wouldn't work including the problem of neighborhood raccoons and cats trying to catch and eat them as a tasty snack while foraging for more edibles ... But she told him to give it a try.

The pet store had a marvelous aquarium filled with the most beautiful goldfish and neon tetras. He felt like a kid in a candy store as he pointed out his choices and the helper would snag them with a small scoop net and place them in a container of water. Stanley didn't feel that his plans for the fish were anybody's business, so when the helper inquired how large the aquarium at home was so he could be sure it could handle his purchases, Stanley just answered, "Very, very big."

A couple of bottles of fish food rounded out his buying trip and returning home he showed Mrs. Betts his treasures. She had to admit they were very beautiful and maybe his hair-brained idea might work out after all. Stanley gently released the fish into the hot tub and enjoyed watching them swim around and explore their new home.

Now to invite the grandkids over for a fabulous surprise. Families are very busy these days, even in the summer time, so it was a day or two before the kids could come over and visit their grandparents. Stanley reminded them to bring their swimsuits whetting their interests by saying in an evasive manner, "You will be in for something very, very special."

Later in the day after he talked with the kids he went out to the hot tub to sprinkle some fish food for his new pets.

Oh no! They were all gone! He was a little concerned that the chlorine in the tub might make his fish sick so he put in extra water; but if this proved to be true they would be floating around with their white tummies up.

Stanley sat down on the porch swing in total dismay. What could have happened? He was sure he didn't notice any cats or raccoons lurking around the backyard. He heard that sometimes birds like falcons, herons or osprey would swoop down and snatch fish off the surface of rivers and lakes but this was even harder to believe. The kids were coming over to splash around in the hot tub … and now his gold fish idea would not happen.

Mrs. Betts peered out the kitchen window and asked, "Are you okay Stanley? You look like you are having more constipation issues."

He turned to Mrs. Betts with a look of total dismay and responded, "All the goldfish are gone.
I don't know what happened?"

Less than sympathetic, she finished the conversation, "I told you it wouldn't work out very well. The kids are coming over and you promised them 'something special.' You better run down to the grocery store and get some popsicles or some other treat."

(Editor's note: The mystery of the missing goldfish was never solved. Much later in the year when Skip at the hot tub repair shop came to replace the water filter and check the lines for leaks or other problems, he looked over the circulation pump and noticed it seemed to have some residue in it that was affecting it's efficiency. As he was cleaning the mechanism he was surprised to see something he had never seen in a hot tub before. It looked like very small fish bones. Nah, that can't be possible. It must be grass or some other stuff that blew into the hot tub over the summer.)

CHAPTER 10

And 'Ducky' Did Come Back

Winters in the Pacific Northwest are as different as the geography. Cities and towns along the Pacific Ocean get lots of rain the whole season. A few snowflakes causes panic among the population because they don't know how to drive on slippery streets. The nearby mountains to the east receive so much snow it is measured in feet rather than inches and sometimes the highway passes are closed to traffic for extended periods of time while the snowplows clear the roads. Further east from the mountains is a vast area called "The Inland Empire." The winter weather there is different each year. Sometimes it is rather mild and pleasant. That's when everyone worries about "global warming." Sometimes there is so much snow people are sick of it by January. Mrs. Betts' yard tells the story in easy terms. The bird baths freeze over and look like little round skating rinks. As of this writing nobody has seen a squirrel in ice skates but anything is possible. The yard and garden is covered with a fluffy blanket of snow that protects everything until springtime opens up its sleepy eyes. Stanley buys a big bag of unsalted peanuts in the shell and occasionally spreads them out under a tree to be sure the squirrels have something to eat. And the winter slowly walks toward warmer weather.

(Editor's note: Thanks for the weather report. We want to know about "Ducky"!)

Mrs. Betts likes to have the bedroom window open a little bit during the night. Sometimes Stanley will get up after she is asleep and close it. Other times he puts on a pair of sox, pulls the covers up to his chin and hopes he won't be a frozen pop sickle by morning.

One early spring morning the last of the winter's snow had melted when Mrs. Betts is awakened by a familiar quacking sound. She walked over to the open window and saw a sight of great delight. It's Ducky!" He had returned after flying south for the winter and he had a friend with him: A smaller grey and light brown pintail duck that is clearly a female.

"Stanley! Wake up!" she calls. "Ducky has come back home."

Stanley pulls the covers up around his neck and mumbles, "If you feel lucky drive over to the Indian casino."

"Not 'lucky'," Mrs. Betts responds, "Ducky!"

Stanley rubs his sleepy eyes, rolls over toward the window, puts on his slippers, and shuffles over to Mrs. Betts. It is probably the first time in his life he has done four things in a row so early in the morning. Sure enough, he sees the family pet enjoying the koi pond and is filled with delight.

Mrs. Betts orders, "Quick! Pop some popcorn while I slice up a couple apples. We know Ducky loves those treats and we want to let him know we are happy he is back."

In short order Stanley takes a bowl of popcorn and a saucer of apple slices over to the slider to the patio. He peers out, then turns to Mrs. Betts, "I don't want to scare away Ducky's friend. I will try to sneak over to the patio steps, sit down, and quietly call to him."

Didn't work. Ducky immediately saw Stanley, splashed out of the koi pond and ran to him quacking happily. Stanley sat down on the steps and Ducky began rubbing his head on his pajama leg making a noise that sounded more like purring than quacking. As Stanley began feeding the treats to Ducky his friend quietly slipped out of the koi pond and began to hide in the nearby bushes. Ducky looked at her and said "Quack-quack." (Which is duck talk for "Get over here fraidy cat. I want you to meet my peeps."

Such a happy time continued into the warm spring days. Ducky's friend got used to Mrs. Betts and Stanley and was waiting with him at the patio slider each morning for their special treats. Since she was now a member of the family, Mrs. Betts thought they should think up a name for her. Stanley suggested "Quack-ette", but this did not set too well, so the little lady duck was finally named: "Daisy." As Mrs. Betts began preparing her garden for another year the ducks would follow her around and find the worms and bugs she dug up getting the soil ready for planting. They both proved to be excellent pets and the cats knew to keep their distance. One bite from Ducky and the word got around to the cats to steer clear.

Well, as usual, things were going too well.

Officer Krupke did not like the quacking noise coming from Mrs. Betts' backyard. He was annoyed when she had a backyard full of penguin sounds and when the crows took over the neighborhood (See Chapter 1 and Chapter 4 for the whole story), and he felt this was even nosier. He saw Stanley out in the backyard and growled, "What's with all the quacking sounds? This is supposed to be a quiet neighborhood. What are you two up to now?"

Stanley happily answered, "Our pet Ducky came home after flying south for the winter and he brought a friend with him we are calling 'Daisy.' With any luck we will have a family of ducks living with us later this summer."

This did not set well with Officer Krupke … at all! He could picture his neighbor's yard swarming with baby ducks that would sneak under his fence and leave poop all over his backyard and patio. Then the thought of the quacking multiplying itself each time a new duck arrived pushed him over the edge. He stormed down to city hall and demanded to see an inspector. "Do we have any city ordinances about raising ducks in the city limits?"

The inspector went over the ordinance books trying to answer his question. "Hmm," he responded, "I guess the question has never come up before. I do see an ordinance against raising chickens within the city limits, if that will help."

Of course, it didn't.

Officer Krupke thought he would try a bluff. Later that day he walked over to the Betts' home and rang the doorbell. Mrs. Betts saw him at the door and brought him a couple of the warm cinnamon rolls she had just taken out of the oven. "It's always nice to see our neighbors," she said in a friendly fashion.

"I'm afraid this isn't a cordial visit," Officer Krupke responded. "I found out that there is an ordinance against raising ducks within the city limits. If this is your plan you will be cited and receive a heavy fine. You might think about that before you get any more ducks on your property. And thanks for the cinnamon rolls."

Mrs. Betts couldn't believe what she had just heard. As Officer Krupke walked back down the front steps, she called to Stanley and told him everything. Frankly, Stanley didn't like his crabby neighbor that much. "I'm having a hard time believing that. I think I will call city hall right now and find out if that is the truth."

Stanley called, and when he was connected with the inspector, the city employee answered, "That's kind of strange. Another person came by this morning and asked the same question. I found out that you can't raise chickens in the city limits, but there isn't anything about raising ducks."

"Thank you for the information," Stanley responded. "That helps a lot. And thank you for your service."

Stanley smiled and told Mrs. Betts what he had just learned. She stormed out the front door, hurried over to Officer Krupke's home and knocked on his door. When he opened it she said frankly, "We found out that there is no problem raising ducks in the city limits. And give me back my cinnamon rolls!"

CHAPTER 11

Power to the People

One cold winter day Stanley waded through the snow to the mailbox to see if anything interesting had arrived. He had been waiting to receive the next issue of the "When Does Old Enough to Know Better Kick In" magazine which he enjoyed reading from cover to cover. Alas, the only items in the mailbox were the usual monthly bills that seem to never end.

Plopping down in his tattered old easy chair in the living room he looked through the mail and decided to open the bill from the power and light company. Because of the cold weather the amount on the bill was always much higher than during the summer and every winter month it seemed to grow larger and larger. Stanley let out a moan of discouragement as he saw how much he and Mrs. Betts would have to pay this time. He looked at his wife and complained, "If this keeps up, I'm going to have to find a job. I had kind of hoped that I could stay retired."

Mrs. Betts was always positive about every situation and answered, "Now Stanley, let's not worry about it. There are lots of things we can do to lessen our power bill. I heard about something called location conservation where people close the heating outlets and shut the doors to rooms in their homes that they never use. We don't spend much time in the downstairs bedroom or in the basement, so why should we keep heating them. I bet that would be a very helpful savings. We could turn down the furnace thermostat a couple degrees and wear sweaters during that day. That would certainly make it better. At night time we could turn the thermostat down even lower and throw an extra blanket on the bed. It would be real cozy."

Stanley had to agree that all three ideas might help, but the thought of wearing itchy wool sweaters all winter just didn't set right with him. Each of their cats had claimed his or her own bedroom and to force them to hang out together would eventually probably result in the next World War as they battled for who would be 'top dog' cat among the four of them. Having their own beds to themselves had made things much easier in the cat competition wars.

Stanley took a drive down to Home Depot to see how much it would cost to put new storm windows on the house. He heard that a lot of heat is lost through older windows and there was no doubt their windows were old. While visiting with the salesman he heard another customer talking about what he had done to deal with the cost of winter heating. He erected a wind-turbine power generator on his property. Not only did this help with his power bill, but on especially windy days the wind mill generated so much electricity he could SELL the extra back to the power and light company. Wow! The best of all worlds!

Stanley hurried home and went straight to 'google'. "Wind power generating," he ordered. 'Google' lightened up and then a long list of possible sources for wind power equipment popped up. "Hmm," Stanley put on his reading glasses and continued, "One of the blades on a wind power turbine are … Hmm, let me write this down … 116 inches. That would be about 10 feet. We would need four blades. The tower to attach the blades would be 212 inches. That would be 17 or 18 feet. Not a problem at all. It looks like everything is white colored. Phyllis would have a fun time painting flowers on the blades and they would blend nicely into her backyard décor. I'm going for it! I don't think I will tell her until the equipment shows up. It will be a fun surprise."

Mrs. Betts walked into the office as Stanley was writing down the phone number of the company that had the best price for his wind-turbine. "What are you up to, Sweet pea?" she asked in a friendly, but curious nature. "Did you find out how much it would cost to put better windows in the house?"

He quickly turned off his computer. "Yes I did, Honey Pot." He answered. "I don't know if we can afford to do it. To update all our windows was so much we would have to get a home loan from the credit union."

"Well, I am willing to do it. In the long run we would get our money back from the savings on our bill from the power and light company." She offered.

Stanley had to admit her suggestion was probably true. "I am looking at some other possibilities, but you might be right. Let's think on it while I do some research on other ways to save energy."

Mrs. Betts smiled and turned heading for the kitchen. "While you do some looking around I will put on the tea kettle. It's almost time for 'Jeopardy'."

Stanley quickly dialed the number of the wind-turbine company.

"Arms of Power Wind-turbines Incorporated. Here's your chance to tell the electric company to take a hike. Jensen speaking."

"Mr. Jensen," Stanley excitedly spoke into his cell phone. "My name is Stanley. We live in a pleasant 4-bedroom house across the street from a busy middle school in a quiet neighborhood of a friendly Pacific Northwest town."

(Editor's note: Where have we heard that before?)

I want to order the GE 1.5 megawatt wind turbine for my property. How soon can you deliver it and set it up."

The salesman was surprised he was going to make such an easy deal. "Shouldn't we talk about the expenses and all the other factors involved. You have to get a permit from the city and they have to come out to check where you plan to erect it to make sure it is safe. Sometimes we have to clear the issue with the neighbors or they will sue us … and you."

Stanley was totally confident there wouldn't be any problems. "You go ahead and make the shipping arrangements. I will clear everything here on my end."

"Well," Mr. Jensen responded. "Stanley, welcome to the Arms of Power family. You can expect your new wind-turbine within a few weeks. We can work out a payment schedule within your budget. Thank you so much for your business."

Stanley was almost as excited as when the Seattle Seahawks won the Super Bowl when he walked out on the back patio to decide the best place for his wind-turbine. He and Mrs. Betts had taken out some old shrubs that were growing next to the fence by Mrs. Malone's property and the bare spot there definitely needed something. This would be absolutely perfect.

Early one winter morning a few weeks later. The growling motor of a big truck woke up Mrs. Betts and Stanley. Then they heard a second truck … then a third truck … Oh my gosh! Then a fourth truck and a fifth truck! Stanley jumped out of bed like a lit rocket. He looked out the front room window and five massive trucks were idling in the street by the house. They were so big he couldn't see them all. Some of the neighbors were bundled up standing on their front porches wondering what the heck was going on.

Stanley quickly dressed and hustled out to the driver of the closest truck.

"Are you Stanley?" the driver asked. "We have your wind turbine."

Stanley could barely respond. "There must be some mistake. These things are huge!"

The driver kind of chuckled. "No. All the wind-turbines are the same size. The blades are 116 feet long and the tower is 212 feet high. All together it stands 328 feet from the ground to the tip of the tallest blade. Each truck carries one blade and the extra truck carries the tower."

Stanley stumbled back as Mrs. Betts arrived on the scene. "I thought the sizes were in INCHES not FEET!"

(Editor's note: Fear not, dear readers. When the power and light company found out what Stanley was trying to do, they thought the best idea would be to buy the wind-turbine so they would still have a monopoly on all the electric power in the city. They had the trucks take the pieces of the wind-turbine to a large empty lot on the outskirts of town where their employees erected it in short order. It proved to be such a great source for electric power they bought a half-dozen more.)

CHAPTER 12

The Mower Growler

There has been a magazine around for many years called *Popular Mechanics*. It published interesting articles like "How to Build Your Own 'Whack-a-Mole Game" or "Say Goodbye to Ants and Cockroaches" or "Save Your Toenail Clippings for Your Garden" or the very popular "How to Make an Atomic Bomb out of Items Found in a Normal American Kitchen." Needless to say Stanley enjoyed reading the magazine and he had owned a monthly subscription for many years. As he was relaxing on the back patio looking over the latest issue, he saw an advertisement that caught his eye: "Now You Too Can be the Proud Owner of a Computer-Operated and Solar Powered Lawn Mower ... Meet 'The Mower Growler. Only $899.00.'"

As mentioned a number of times earlier in this story Stanley and Mrs. Betts shared the responsibilities for keeping their property looking like something out of a lawn contest winner from *Sunset Magazine*. Mrs. Betts was the expert on flowers and other decorative plants and Stanley kept the grass nicely mowed and also the weeds under control. As the years went by it was getting more and more difficult on his lower back to mow the lawn, but he never complained and always did what needed to be done. The idea of having a computer-operated lawn mower really intrigued him. According to the advertisement all the owner needed to do was to program the mower so it would know where to mow and how short to cut the grass. Then push the 'start' button and sit back and relax. Boy did that sound good!

There was a photo of the lawn mower and it was a very impressive iridescent green color with four large narrow round tires, a number of panels of solar batteries, a motor that could have operated a small car, and a very complicated looking computer system with a built-in keyboard and screen. It had its own headlight so it could work at night and a number of small blue electric lights sprinkled around for effect. There was an adjustable handle and a small flat area attached so the mini-drone, about the size of a robin, that guided it would have a place to take off and land. The finishing touches were two big eyes and a mouth full of teeth painted on the front of the contraption. That probably explained the "Growler" name. It kind of looked like an angry square green lion.

Stanley folded back the page of the magazine, admired the lawn mower for the longest time, then said under his breath, "I've got to have that! I want The Mower Growler."

Now the next steps toward getting his new toy was to convince Mrs. Betts that it was a good idea. As you can see by the price listed in the ad, the computer-operated lawn mower was very expensive for retired people or actually for anybody. It did come with a three year all-inclusive repair warrantee and a "if you don't like it you can return it within 30 days of purchase for a full refund' enticement. Stanley thought, "What can go wrong?"

Editor's note: Haven't we heard this before? 'What can go wrong?' usually means something is bound to go wrong.

Stanley knew getting Mrs. Betts to support his idea was not going to be easy so he began to design a five-step plan:

- Step one … Mention to Mrs. Betts that the lawn mower they had was getting old and didn't really do that good of a job cutting the grass anymore.

- Step two … After the next few times he mowed the lawn start complaining a little that he had a back ache. To make it seem a little more serious maybe sit in the hot tub after the jobs and moan a little.

- Step three … Mention that maybe they didn't have to go on a long and expensive vacation this year. A weekend or two at the lake would be more than adequate. This would imply that they might have a little extra money on hand.

- Step four … Let Mrs. Betts know that he was thinking about selling some of his many, many baseball card collections. Saying in passing that after so many years it was getting kind of boring to continue gathering baseball cards.

- Step five … Then, leave the *Popular Mechanics* magazine with the information about the computer-operated lawn mower on the coffee table in the living room or on the night stand in the bedroom. Of course, opened to the advertisement about the "Mower

Growler." Mrs. Betts might accidentally notice it and read about how 'cool' it was and that if would help Stanley's sore back.

Stanley had to admit that putting his entire plan into effect might take a month or so, but he was determined to stick with it as long as he could. At the most it might mean three or four more lawn mowing jobs and he could handle that okay.

One morning sometime later as Stanley and Mrs. Betts were sitting on the patio enjoying their warm steaming coffee, Mrs. Betts mentioned something that really made Stanley sit up in suppressed joy. "Stanley," Mrs. Betts started, "I was looking at one of your *Popular Mechanics* magazines and saw an advertisement that really caught my eye. It talked about a computer-operated lawn mower. Can you imagine that?"

This was Stanley's chance to strike. "I saw that too! Do you think we could use something like that? If it works like the ad said, I could do other people's lawns besides ours and bring home a little extra money."

Bingo!

So Stanley ordered his Mower Growler. The company that made the machines was having trouble selling them, so when they connected with Stanley they gave him a 20% discount and free shipping. Every day he would watch for the big brown UPS delivery truck in hopes it would pull into the driveway. And one day it did! And it was one of the big UPS delivery trucks. Stanley stepped out the front door as two strong young men in their brown uniforms climbed out of the truck and asked if he were Stanley. When he identified himself they opened up the back of their truck and wrestled out a massively large orange cardboard box that had the words "Get 'em!" printed on the side. Clearly, they were eager to get the load out of the truck and in minutes drove away to continue their deliveries.

Mrs. Betts joined Stanley on the driveway and they began unpacking their precious cargo. Wow! It really was an impressive piece of machinery! Stanley found the owner's manual and began reading how to get it going. The first statement printed in the manual said simply:

"We recommend that you enlist the help of a professional computer programmer to get the Mower Growler ready for work."

Stanley ignored those words confident that he could figure it out since he was comfortable with his lap top in the office.

The first procedure involved getting the mini-drone going. Apparently it had some communication system with the lawn mower and as it cruised along sent back photos of the landscape. The plan was that the mower would add them into its memory bank and would then know where to go. The mini-drone had its own set of controls and did not appear to be too complicated. Once Stanley had the battery charged he started it up and it hummed like a little honey bee. It was smaller than a model airplane and had four propellers buzzing comfortably. He slowly pushed the 'go' switches and it gracefully rose above the landing pad on the mower and hovered silently waiting for the next command.

Oh oh!

Lucky the Cat was watching everything from under a nearby bush and when he saw the small drone starting to fly he was sure it was some kind of bird and attacked it with all his might. He jumped onto the mower then leaped into the air and crashed against the drone. It trickled to the ground in a dozen pieces and the four propellers flew off in the direction of the middle school across the street.

Stanley and Mrs. Betts could not believe their eyes! Lucky the Cat was so shocked he ducked back under the bush where he had been hiding and didn't come out the rest of the day.

Stanley sat on the front steps with the owner's manual in his lap almost in tears. He began to thumb through the manual and found a section that said "What to do if the drone malfunctions." Well, it was worth a try. The manual said that the Mower Growler actually had its own guidance system and with some reprogramming could find itself around a yard with little or no trouble. Then a long list of instructions followed. Stanley scanned the list in confusion. "CTL-ALT-DEL?" "PGUP?" "PGDN?" "PRTSC?" He had no idea what all those meant or even if they were on a computer keyboard. It was "SYSRO" that pushed him over the edge. Totally deflated he just sat there as the owner's manual dropped off his lap and quietly bounced down the stairs to the sidewalk.

Mrs. Betts saw how dejected Stanley looked and sat down beside him and started rubbing his shoulders. "It will be okay. We must know somebody who is comfortable with computers. Let's try to think of someone then ask if he or she would be willing to come over and look at the situation."

Of course! Who else except Garry Richards? Stanley and Mrs. Betts had known the Richards for years and Garry had actually worked in computer programming for the U.S. Postal Service. One phone call and Garry was eager to get involved. He had seen the ad for the Mower Growler in his own copy of *Popular Mechanics* and had discussed the idea with his wife Cheryl. When Mrs. Betts found out he was coming over she began preparing a nice lunch and asked Stanley to call him back to see if his wife could come also.

In short order the Richards arrived and Garry begin reading the owner's manual as Stanley, Mrs. Betts and Cheryl brought out some lawn chairs and watched him closely. Some of the neighbors wondered what was going on and pretty soon there was a half-dozen or more people on the scene. Mrs. Betts had Stanley find some more chairs and everyone was comfortable and very, very interested.

Garry found the 'on' button and the marvelous machine roared into life growling like a hungry lion. The computer screen began glowing with the words "Ready for Action."

Garry said, "That's a good sign. I think we are going to be in business." Studying the owner's manual he began to type commands into the machine through the keyboard.

The Mower Growler began trembling almost as if it were excited to get to work. Everyone moved their chairs back a few feet to feel a little bit safer.

"Here we go!" Garry yelled, then pushed the blinking 'go' button. The Mower Growler started slowly spinning in a circle and everyone ran for the safety of the front steps!

Then it just took off in a random direction!

It roared across 23rd Avenue, chewed its way through the chain link fence of the school yard and then mowed a single strip clear across the playfield toward the school building! When it bumped against the building it turned left 90 degrees, mowed a path to Skipworth Street and took off like a rocket on up the road. Stanley and Garry jumped into Garry's jeep and tried to catch up with it so they could turn it off. Too late! The Mower Growler easily broke through the fence along the Interstate Highway, bounced onto the pavement, turned east and disappeared in a cloud of dust and concrete. The mower company had advertised that the solar batteries could keep it running forever and that is just what happened.

The last we heard was that it was on Interstate Highway 86 about 20 miles west of Pocatello, Idaho, and the Idaho Highway Patrol was following it with their lights flashing and their sirens screaming to alert people to clear out of the way.

CHAPTER 13

Garden Gnomes ... from Nome?

As you are aware by now, Mrs. Betts was always looking for ways to make her famous backyard even more interesting and attractive.

One spring morning Mrs. Betts asked Stanley, "Would you like to go for a walk around the block and see what the neighbors are doing with their yards? Maybe we might see something that we would like to add to our property."

Stanley looked up from the television and mumbled, "I don't even want to 'rock around the clock' leastways walk around the block."

"Oh come on, lazy boy," Mrs. Betts chided. "A little exercise wouldn't hurt you at all, and I would enjoy your company."

Stanley had to admit it was a beautiful day and who knows what they might see. The neighborhood was always the showplace of that part of town when it came to yards and gardens so they strolled comfortably along and enjoyed the sights. On the corner was the home of Mrs. Fuddpucker. The kids called her "Mrs. Funwrecker" because she was so crabby. She would sit on her front porch with a cup of coffee and a broom across her lap and when they would ride by on their bicycles she would say, "Keep out of my yard or I will sick Bruno on you." Bruno was this monstrous tom cat that easily weighed 40 pounds and looked more like a small tiger than a cat. He would sit by Mrs. Fuddpucker and hope she would let him attack anybody that came by. Stories were shared around the neighborhood about Bruno shredding bike tires and kids' tennis shoes. Despite her dislike for anyone under four feet tall, she was generally civil to the adults should they come by.

As Stanley and Mrs. Betts approached her home they saw her working in the front yard. She was placing the most amazing item among her daffodils. It was a small clay statue of a gnome about a foot or two tall … and very, very colorful. Mrs. Betts was intrigued and inquired, "Gladys, where did you get that garden gnome. It is beautiful!"

Responding to the compliment, and ordering Bruno to "Stay!" she mentioned that Home Depot had just received a large shipment of garden gnomes … maybe from Nome, Alaska, and they were on sale. Where they actually came from is debatable but it seemed logical to her that gnomes should come from Nome, Alaska.

That was all Mrs. Betts needed to hear. "Back to the house and get the truck keys, Stanley. We are off to Home Depot!"

The display of garden gnomes at Home Depot was unbelievable to see. Every size, color, and shape was on sale … and going fast. Almost every shopping cart on the property had at least one garden gnome riding among the bags of fertilizer and potting soil. "Get a cart, quick!" Mrs. Betts ordered. "We have to get some of them before they are all gone."

As Stanley wandered off to find a shopping cart, he thought, "If I take a little extra time maybe they will all be sold out."

Not a chance!

By the time Stanley and Mrs. Betts loaded up the pickup truck with garden gnomes, the bed of the truck looked more like a miniature circus. There were boy gnomes, girl gnomes, sitting gnomes, standing gnomes, lying down gnomes … and who know what else? All were painted in the brightest and most shocking color combinations. A person would have to put on sun glasses to look at all of them at once.

Mrs. Betts was ecstatic! She couldn't wait to get home and sprinkle them around her yard … and maybe go back to Home Depot and get another load. Garden gnomes are usually made of clay and are pretty heavy, so Stanley knew what was in store for him. Mrs. Betts would decide where to place them … and he would have to do it, so he got his wheelbarrow out of the shed and stood at the ready.

Mrs. Betts sat down at the kitchen table and began to draw a map of her back yard. She had made a list of the gnomes on hand and tried to decide how best to display them: By color, whether they were standing, sitting, or lying down, similar sizes? The possibilities were endless.

Stanley was hoping to delay the process so he gave a not so serious suggestion, "How about organizing them like small families? Find a lady gnome, a man gnome, and a couple of kid gnomes and put them somewhere in the yard as a group. You have plenty of oil paints, so you could actually paint their clothes so they look they go together."

"Brilliant!" she responded. "Sometimes you really surprise me! Unload the gnomes onto the garage floor while I go get my paints. This is going to be spectacular!"

Stanley smiled to himself as he walked out to the pickup truck. He was pretty sure it would take Mrs. Betts hours to decide how to group the gnomes and what colors to paint them. Then, of course, they couldn't be moved until the paint dried. There was a good chance the placing of the gnomes would have to wait until tomorrow … and with any luck he would die of a heart attack sometime during the night.

Not a chance!

(Editor's note: You are getting redundant. Have you thought about taking a class on basic writing techniques from the local Community College?)

The next morning Stanley was awaken by the sounds of doors opening and closing and scraping sounds from the garage. Still in his slippers and robe he walked outside to see that Mrs. Betts had arranged her freshly painted gnomes into families. Each group had a number written on cardboard next to that selection. He had to admit they really looked much better than they did before. Some of the earlier paint was chipped off from shipping and all those white spots had been covered by new paint.

"Stanley! I'm glad you're here." she said. "You will notice I numbered each group of gnomes. If you go around and look at the backyard, you will see the same numbers on cardboard spread around the flower beds and near the koi pond. That will tell you where to put each family. Once you use your wheelbarrow to get the gnomes there and unload them at the appropriate location, I will arrange the families the ways I have in mind. Now, darling, get to work!"

Stanley gave Mrs. Betts his best 'stink eye'. "Do you mind if I get dressed first," he responded and not too kindly.

"Of course, dear," Mrs. Betts answered. "Just don't take too long. I'm on a roll."

Dressed and ready for work, Stanley began loading up groups of gnomes on his wheelbarrow and taking them to the designated locations. Mrs. Betts would organize the families in an artistic and pleasant fashion and as she worked the backyard was transforming into a magical fairy land.

As what seems to happen more and more often to the Betts household, things were going too well and disaster was looming on the horizon.

Ducky and Daisy lazily climbed out of their nest by the koi pond and Ducky went 'bananas!' He didn't know who the strangers were in his backyard, but he didn't like it at all. As far as he knew these interlopers were dangerous and he had to protect his lady friend in hopes of having a family of ducklings. Waving his wings and quacking wildly he attacked the nearest garden gnome and it broke in half. He stomped on it with his wide webbed feet and it shattered into a kaleidoscope of colors and pieces. Satisfied that he had killed it off, he turned and ran toward his next target.

Mrs. Betts screamed, "Ducky! Stop it! They won't hurt you! Stanley, get the garden hose and blast him. He's out of his mind!"

Ducky had been the family pet for quite a while and he had experienced the 'garden hose punishment' on prior occasions when he misbehaved. When he saw Stanley go for it, he realized there was a small chance he might be a little out of line so he stopped in his tracks and looked at Mrs. Betts for instructions.

Mrs. Betts gently picked him up and spoke softly, "Ducky, these are like toys that you shouldn't play with. If they really bother you, we will take them back to the store." She held him in her arms for a moment then placed him back on the ground. He looked at her, quacked wildly, flapped his wings, and went for another garden gnome. By then Stanley had the hose spraying in Ducky's direction so he broke off the attack and headed back to his nest. Daisy followed him back into the bushes and things quieted down quickly.

Mrs. Betts sat down in a folding chair on the patio clearly very distressed and confused.

Stanley sat next to her and said quietly, "It looks like it is either going to be Ducky and Daisy or garden gnomes. I wouldn't be surprised that if we go in the house, he will run out and break more of them."

Mrs. Betts thought for a few moments then replied, "I suppose we could put a few of them in the front yard, but there just isn't enough room for all the ones we have. I worked so hard to paint them and make them look nice. What if Home Depot won't take them back."

Stanley tried to inject a little humor in the situation, "Christmas presents?" The stormy look she gave him clearly indicated his timing was a little off. He got his wheelbarrow and began loading up the pickup with the garden gnomes. This was a sad moment for Mrs. Betts. She had great plans for her backyard and was sure she would win the Garden of the Month Award once she had everything ready.

(Editor's note: Fear not dear readers, this chapter also has a happy ending.)

When they returned to Home Depot with the load of gnomes the garden department manager saw how beautifully painted they were so he accepted them graciously. Then he asked Mrs. Betts if she would be willing to bring her paints to the store and repair the gnomes that had been chipped or cracked. He said, she would be paid for it of course.

If you stop by the Betts' house the next few weeks there won't be anybody at home. Mrs. Betts will be repairing

and painting garden gnomes, and Stanley will be mum-
bling to himself saying something about he thought
slavery was illegal as he puts them back on the shelves.

CHAPTER 14

Hug a Tree – Save a Squirrel

Before the Betts family had their nice home built some 35 years ago the property was a grove of ponderosa pine trees some as tall as 50 feet or more. The house construction company wanted to cut them all down and sell the trees for lumber, but Mrs. Betts convinced them to only cut down the trees that might be in the way of actually building the home and the plans for the front and back yards. She appreciated the shade that trees made and wanted to have as many as possible to keep the hot sun away during the summer time.

As the years walked onward, the remaining trees continued to grow and some were easily 70 or 80 feet tall. Despite the fact that every fall and winter they covered the yard and roof of the house with pine needles Mrs. Betts thought it was a fair trade for what the trees offered keeping the property comfortable. Each year Stanley liked the trees less and less as he was the one who had to rake the pine needles, sweep them off the roof and clean them out of the koi pond more than once each year and take them to the recycling center in his pickup. He did like that the squirrels had made their homes in the trees and watching them frolic around the yard made him laugh. He always had a bag of salt-free peanuts in the shell to give them now and then.

One day, Mrs. Betts had the tree trimmers come to cut away the dead branches and generally tidy up the trees and bushes. This happened every couple of years and everything looked so much nicer by the time they had finished. They always hauled away the branches and limbs so Stanley didn't have to deal with them. One of the trimmers called Mrs. Betts out to the backyard and shared a concern he found while doing the job on one of the larger ponderosa pine trees. "Mrs. Betts," he said. "Take a look at the trunk of this pine tree. Do you see it appears that the beginnings of a hole is developing right about eye-level. As you scan up the tree trunk you will see large lumps of dried sap. Sometimes this tells us that the interior of the tree may be starting to rot and holes are developing in the bark. It's the tree's way of healing itself. If this is the case a strong wind might cause it to break off. Then you know what would happen next. Either it would destroy your roof or knock the neighbor's fence over. Whatever, it could be a serious problem."

Mrs. Betts thought a minute and asked, "What do you think we should do about it?"

The worker answered, "I would recommend you hire us to take it down. We have trained tree removers and the equipment to take care of the problem quickly and neatly."

"Just how serious is it?" Mrs. Betts continued.

"Let me get my tool. I will drill a small hole in the trunk and take out a sample of the heart wood."

Mrs. Betts and Stanley watched the worker as he did the job. He put a long drill bit on his equipment and began to push it into the tree trunk. In a brief moment it suddenly went in very easily, a sign that it was becoming hollow in the middle. The wood that came out with the drill bit looked like sawdust as it crumbled and scattered on the ground. "Doesn't look too good to me," the man commented.

After the tree trimming company people left for the day, Mrs. Betts and Stanley had a serious issue to talk about. "What do you think, Stanley," Mrs. Betts asked.

"I don't know. The tree looks strong and healthy to me. The tree trunk is so big that if I tried to stretch my arms around it there would still be a lot of tree left over. In fact, I don't think the two of us working together could sur-round the whole tree," Stanley answered. "And a family of squirrels with a new batch of babies have made their home in that tree. Remember, these tree trimming com-panies make their living cutting down people's trees and selling the wood to be turned in to lumber or fire wood. I don't think we should worry about it."

Mrs. Betts has always been the level headed person in the family. She tries to anticipate problems and find ways to avoid them before they happen. "What if the tree goes down like the worker said? I feel it would be best to have them come and take care of it. We have lots of other trees so it won't be missed. I think I will phone the company to-morrow and make an appointment to have them come out."

Stanley sat up in his chair, "What about the squirrel fam-ily and all their little babies?"

Mrs. Betts didn't respond. She had made up her mind … and that was that.

Early the next morning Stanley devised a plan of action. He was not going to allow anybody to cut down that tree until the babies were old enough to live on their own. Mrs. Betts was enjoying her coffee and watching the morning news on the local TV station. The weather lady said to be prepared for 50 to 60 mile an hour wind gusts for the day. "Be sure to close down your patio umbrellas," she said cutely.

Mrs. Betts heard Stanley rustling around in the garage, but didn't give it a second thought. He decided he would chain himself to the tree to keep anybody from cutting it down. He put on his overcoat, found a chain and lock, put a chair against the tree and settled in. He spread some peanuts around the tree so the squirrels would come out and be part of the scene. His protest would not have much effect unless people found out about it, so without telling Mrs. Betts his plan he called the TV station on his cell phone and gave them an anonymous tip: "There's a man by the junior high school at 11322 E. 23rd Avenue who has chained himself to a tree to keep anybody from cutting it down. You should come out and see what is going on."

The winds had started up and were howling in the trees and a few rain drops were dancing along with the wind gusts. In a brief time the television company's bright van rolled up to the Betts' home and parked near the front yard. The roof slid open and a narrow metal rod with a small satellite dish began to unfold and slowly climb above the vehicle. Wow! This was not going to be some "Pictures at 11" news item. Apparently this was important enough that it was going to be a "On the spot! What's happening now!" news story. Mrs. Betts looked out the living room window and saw what was happening. She decided they were probably getting ready to cover some activity at the school across the street.

The news anchorman on the TV said, "We interrupt regular programming to bring you a special bulletin. Our reporter Tammy Tinkle is at the location."

The camera man and a reporter climbed out of the van and the young lady started talking. "This is Tammy Tinkle and I am here to find out what in the world is going on." She continued explaining what the TV station knew at this point. Mrs. Betts mouth dropped open. The woman on her TV screen was the same one in her front yard!

Of course, many of the neighbors were watching the same morning news so when they realized it was happening right next door this caused quite a commotion and they put on their coats, and despite the growing wind storm, began collecting around the Betts' house to see what was going on first hand. The local newspaper had been watching the event on their TV so they sent a reporter and photographer out to the Betts' house to capture the story.

Mrs. Betts ran to the back slider, peered out at Stanley chained to the tree and could not believe her eyes. "Stanley! What in the 'H-E-double toothpicks' are you doing?"

(Editor's note: "H-E-double toothpicks" is a nicer way of saying "H-E-L-L")

The television camera man and reporter walked across the backyard to where Stanley was situated. The camera was running and the satellite dish was sending the pictures directly to the TV station where the story was being broadcast to a live audience across the entire city. Stanley made sure the camera was facing him and said strongly, "I have just begun to fight. I will not leave this tree until I can be assured it won't be cut down. There is a family of squirrels living in this tree and I will not allow them to be harmed." Then he thought, "Whenever there is some kind of protest on TV the people are chanting something." So he said bravely, "Hug a tree! Save a squirrel. Hug a tree! Save a squirrel!"

The neighbors cheered and clapped their hands and added their voices to the chant as the camera showed them watching the spectacle. The TV station liked it so much they had plans to televise the incident on the 5 o'clock news as well as the 11 o'clock news and put it on their Face Book Page. It had hundreds, if not thousands, of 'likes.' The slogan swept the nation and "Hug a tree! Save a squirrel." ended up on tee shirts and coffee cups from coast to coast.

Mrs. Betts was standing on the patio glaring at Stanley. She did not want to appear to be the 'bad guy' in front of the entire city, but she did not like the way Stanley had put her in the predicament. The newspaper people arrived and the photographer started taking pictures as the reporter interviewed the bystanders. This story was going to be featured on the front page of the next edition.

Thank goodness Mother Nature saves the day:

At that very moment a strong gust of wind swept across the yard and, you guessed it, the tree made a loud cracking noise about 6 feet above the squirrel nest. The TV camera showed everything and the newspaper photographer was taking pictures as fast as he could as the top 50 or 60 feet of the tree trembled then slowly tilted over being pushed cruelly by the driving wind storm. It dropped to the ground and was so heavy it felt like an earthquake right on Officer Krupke's back fence. The fence was smashed to smithereens, the crashing top of the tree was so long it ripped down his power line and cable TV connection, and he had some garden gnomes in his backyard that were nothing more than colorful pieces of clay.

Officer Krupke's face told the whole story. And of course the TV cameraman and the newspaper photographer put their equipment on 'zoom' and the reporter held the microphone in his direction so the whole city could hear his words. "You, you people are the worse neighbors in the world! You are going to pay for everything! And I want a new fence like the one they are building on the Mexican border: 20 feet tall and made of steel." As he headed for the back door, he looked back and said, "And I want barbed wire on the top of my new fence!"

When the crowd heard what Officer Krupke said ... everyone; the TV crew on site and at the station and all the neighbors and newspaper people laughed so hard some of them started to cough. Even Mrs. Betts got over her anger with Stanley.

(Editor's note: Mrs. Betts contacted her home owner's insurance company. They had been watching the program on TV and knew what had happened. The story was featured on the front page of the newspaper and Stanley saved some copies for his scrap book. In just a day or so a tree trimming company was there cleaning up the mess. With chainsaws roaring, they cut the branches off the fallen tree trunk and ran them though the bark chipper. Once the trunk was clear of branches they cut it into round sections in preparation for becoming fire wood and rolled them to a trailer parked on the street. One of the men got out a long ladder and trimmed off the top of the tree still standing on the Betts' property. As he looked at the cut, he saw the inside was hollow so he found a metal trash can lid and placed it over the opening so the squirrels wouldn't get rained on in their nest a few feet below.

Mrs. Betts didn't like the rather tall tree trunk with no branches standing there like a big finger, but decided she could put up with it until the babies moved out. The squirrels didn't like the empty tree trunk without branches for protection either. When it rained the metal trash can cover would make a racket which annoyed everyone in the nest so the daddy squirrel built another home in a nearby tree and moved his family over. It was quite an occasion and Stanley invited the TV station and the newspaper people to come by and take pictures. Which they did happily. The whole city was concerned if the squirrel family was doing okay. Mrs. Betts asked the tree trimmers to stop by and cut what was left of the tree trunk off to the ground level which they were willing to do because it meant a lot more firewood to sell.

The insurance company called the power and light company and the cable TV people and they were quick to repair those damages to Officer Krupke's property. Mrs. Betts' son John knew how to make nice fences, so he built one out of cedar wood about 8 feet high. Officer Krupke was accepting of his work.

A few days later a "For Sale" sign appeared in Officer Krupke's front yard. The entire neighborhood was happy to see it there.

CHAPTER 15

The Battle of Kudzu

Mrs. Betts' backyard had become the topic of conversations all over the entire town. Everyone had read about or seen the story of "Hug a Tree … Save a Squirrel." The newspaper editor wanted to take advantage of the community's interest so he contacted Mrs. Betts and asked if she would be willing to write an article once a month for his newspaper. He said he would call it "Mrs. Betts' Backyard." (*Not so original, eh?*). He made it even more inviting by saying he would have a photographer come out and take some photos to go with her stories.

We all know Mrs. Betts had what was called "a green thumb" which meant she could grow anything anywhere. One of her first articles was about "Food Gardening" and the different kinds of vegetables she planted among her flowers. It became so popular that many people rushed to Home Depot's garden shop to buy vegetable seed packets for their own gardens. Needless to say the employees were very happy with Mrs. Betts for starting this new fad. It made lots of bucks for the company. Like almost everybody, the novice gardeners grew too many kinds of vegetables, even beets. Wondering what to do with the bounty they took the extra items to the local food banks which became flooded with fresh produce at harvest time. Mrs. Betts wrote another article about planting flowers that bloomed every year rather than once a year. The newspaper photographer came out to the backyard and took some beautiful pictures so there was another rush to Home Depot, this time to buy perennial flowers. The store was so happy that they decided to honor Mrs. Betts as "Customer of the Year." She got a nice certificate of appreciation and a thank-you gift of 20 35-pound bags of beauty bark. Stanley had to load them on his pickup, take them home, then unload them and stack them outside the garage. Someone heard him mumble, "She should get a certificate for "Slave Driver of the Year." Her article called "The Joy of Koi" which talked about her koi pond started another rush to Home Depot to find out if they made koi ponds or knew who did.

Far and away her most popular story was "Caring for Ducks and Ducklings." Ducky and Daisy had given birth to three little fuzz ball babies that enjoyed swimming around in the koi pond. She mentioned that there were no ordinances against raising ducks within the city limits and the picture of the ducklings enjoying the koi pond included with her article was so cute that people swarmed to the local pet stores and bought every duckling they had. When the stores ran out of ducklings they offered their customers baby chickens. People didn't know that was against the rules, so the city inspector was busy writing citations for those who tried to raise hens and roosters. The pet stores were so happy with Mrs. Betts they gave her a certificate of appreciation at their annual meeting. She was getting so many certificates that there wasn't any room on her office walls for pictures of the grand kids.

(Editor's note: I hope Mrs. Betts doesn't hurt her shoulder patting herself on the back, but this isn't the first time you titled a chapter then didn't write anything that had to with it. When do you plan to get to the story? Christmas? By the way, what is kudzu anyway?)

(Information note: Kudzu is a sturdy and aggressive vine that was imported from Asia in the late 1800's. It doesn't need much water and can grow in almost any kind of soil so people thought it would be good for controlling erosion and for providing ground cover and food for small animals. It is also called "Virginia Creeper" and spiders especially like to live in it. Kudzu proved to be so invasive that it crawled all across America's southeast and is now quite a problem.)

As we all know, Mrs. Betts loves her backyard. She even won her fourth "Garden of the Month" award recently. (Another certificate of appreciation for her office wall.) The only part of the backyard she wasn't happy with was the corner where Mrs. Malone's fence meets the fence across the south border of the property. Some years ago she planted a flowering cherry tree that grew into a tall and graceful addition to the scene, but the ground around it just couldn't support any flowers. Probably because there wasn't much sunlight and the sprinkler system didn't reach that area. So, she had Stanley cover it with beauty bark which was a yearly chore for him that he didn't exactly enjoy. She decided to get on the internet and research plants that do not need a good supply of both sunlight and water. That's when she discovered kudzu. It seemed like the perfect match and the article said when it flowers the small light blue blooms attract honey bees.

Sometime later a brown UPS truck pulled into the driveway and unloaded a large and very heavy cardboard box. It was her shipment of kudzu plants. "Stanley, get your wheelbarrow and your digging tools! We are going to plant some kudzu!" She called out happily.

Stanley was right in the middle of watching the movie "Lawrence of Arabia" on the Turner Classic Movies channel and was not pleased with the interruption. "Kudzu, Schmudzu. I'm busy." He responded.

"Don't be such an old grump. This will be fun!" She chided.

Well, you guessed it. It wasn't much fun for Stanley but he relented. They carefully dug small holes through the beauty bark and placed the plants in even rows. Then Stanley pulled the garden hose over to the work area, attached a small sprinkler, and gave the hungry plants their first drink since they started their trip. It surprised him how the plants immediately perked up, but he didn't give it a second thought.

The next morning Mrs. Betts took her cup of coffee and walked over to the planting area to see how things were going. She was amazed to see small vines reaching out from the plants like little green fingers in all directions. Obviously her kudzu plants were very happy with their new home. By the end of the day the vines had crawled a foot or so and were growing leaves. A couple of the vines had already started to wrap themselves around the trunk of the flowering cherry tree and others were exploring the fencing for places to hold on. Mrs. Betts could picture that back corner covered with beautiful green foliage and couldn't wait for the blooms to begin.

(Editor's note: Dear readers, are you sensing the beginnings of a problem? You are correct.)

A few days later Stanley cranked up the power lawn mower and was cutting the grass. As he went past the corner where the kudzu was planted vines were already inching over the lawn. He cut them with the lawn mower and it seemed as if the remaining sections of the vines drew back almost as if alive. The roar of the mower motor shut out something that almost sounded like "Ouch" from the heart of the kudzu plants as the beauty bark separated and what looked like an eye peered out. Stanley noticed that and was sure it just a rock or something.

This was just the beginning. A warning letter came from the kudzu plants distributing company informing the customer of how aggressive they were and that they needed constant cutting back or they would take over an entire area and choke out any plants already there. This was becoming very obvious and kept both Mrs. Betts and Stanley busy with their electric trimmers. Almost daily they had to work in the planted area. On one occasion a kudzu plant wrapped its sticky vine around Stanley's ankle and he yelled out in surprise then stomped it into little green pieces. It never happened again and made Stanley wonder if it knew it had done something wrong.

The last straw occurred about a month after the original planting. One of the vines had found a knot hole in the fence and it slipped through and began to creep across

Mrs. Malone's backyard. After a few days she noticed it and found a garden hoe to chop it back to the fence line. As she hacked at the vine it curled around the hoe and seemed to try to jerk it out of her hands. She screamed in dismay and fought like a wildcat to get it to let go. Stanley was trimming some branches in the backyard and quickly ran to the situation. He turned on the trimmer and cut the aggressor into small pieces. Once it got the message it retracted itself back through the knothole with a weird growling sound and left Mrs. Malone and Stanley looking at each other in total shock and disbelief.

Stanley said simply, "I will take care of it. This is now personal."

He went into the house and told Mrs. Betts the whole story. She couldn't believe her ears but did not doubt in the least that it had happened. "What are you going to do" She questioned.

"Round-up Weed and Garden Spray. And lots of it." He replied simply.

With the determination of a man getting ready go to war Stanley found his weapon of choice then he walked down to the closet in the basement and found his old combat boots and military jacket that had been stored there since the Vietnam War. He really looked like a warrior as he stormed out to the backyard where the kudzu had made itself at home. I realize this sounds unbelievable, but when the kudzu plants saw him coming their way they seemed to draw in their vines and cover themselves up for protection. The eye mentioned earlier blinked then seemed to burrow itself into the beauty bark in hopes it would survive. Stanley started singing:

> *"Put silver wings upon my chest*
> *Make me one of America's best*
> *A hundred men may try today*
> *But only three wear the green beret."*

Then he began drowning the kudzu plants with the powerful weed killer. Even today the neighbors talk about the painful moaning sounds that came from Mr. Betts' backyard that pleasant summer afternoon. No weed no matter how powerful can withstand the onslaught of Round-up Weed and Garden Spray. In mere minutes the invasive kudzu plants were merely dried up chunks of vegetation.

Stanley got special pleasure out of pulling the remains of the plants up by their roots and rolling his full wheelbarrow to the concrete pad beside the house until it was trash picking up time.

Mrs. Betts had resigned herself to the fact that the back corner of her yard would forever be void of any plant life … and honestly, she got comfortable with that fact.

CHAPTER 16

Grandkids under Every Rock (or so it seems)

Stanley and Mrs. Betts really enjoyed meeting their first grandchild, Kiara. Stanley was heard to say, "If I knew grandkids were so much fun, I wouldn't have had any kids and would have gone straight to them." Of course, we know that isn't possible.

By the time the fifth grandchild arrived it was still good news but had somewhat lost it's luster. Stanley and Mrs. Betts were on the telephone getting the information and Stanley muttered, "Well now we have a basketball team. I hope they aren't trying for a football team."

Mrs. Betts scowled at him and responded, "What do you mean? There's no such thing as too many grand-children." Of course, she was right.

Editor's note: What's with all the 'of courses.' Haven't I talked to you before about redundancy?
Sorry.

By the time the grandchild assembly-line had stopped Stanley and Mrs. Betts had six grandsons and five grand-daughters. When Fiona joined the happy family Stanley scratched his head and commented, "How about that. We have eleven grandkids. We do have a football team. What's next? A philharmonic orchestra?"

Three of the grandchildren arrived within a month and a half of each other. Stanley called his children to remind them this wasn't some kind of a competition with a blue ribbon waiting for the winner. This comment was not received with any special enthusiasm.

Grandkids loved to come to Stanley and Mrs. Betts' house. And they had the most fun when a number of them showed up at the same time. They all got along and seemed to like each other's company. Mrs. Betts was a remarkable cook and baked the best treats for the little ones to enjoy. Stanley liked this too because he was the official taste tester. Their big 65-inch TV was especially popular and they had lots of kid's channels on their cable TV plan as well as NETFLIX.

"We need some kind of playground equipment for the backyard so the kids will have something to do. I don't want them with their faces in their tablets or watching TV indoors all day." said Mrs. Betts.

I think I will design a couple of horseshoe pits. I like to toss horseshoes and could teach them how to do it," was Stanley's contribution to the plan.

Mrs. Betts just rolled her eyes (again). "You have got to be kidding. You may like to toss horseshoes with some of your friends, but children don't do that anymore. Besides a horseshoe is made out of iron. There's a good chance some of them would hurt themselves"

Stanley thought a moment then added, "How about an archery set. You know, we could set up a big target by the koi pond and they could shoot arrows at it or shoot each other in the eye. Or if you think that is too dangerous I could buy some of those throwing darts. It's just a rumor that kids impale themselves on their sharp points and have to be taken to the hospital in an ambulance."

Mrs. Betts could not believe what he was saying. Of course (*again*) he was just kidding. "I'm thinking of a swing set or a slide."

This was a good idea, but who knows where you can buy a swing set or a slide? Obviously schools and playgrounds have figured that out, but not many individual people are in the market for those items and Toys R Us has closed down. Thank goodness for *Google*. A quick inquiry and two different companies in town sold playground equipment for backyards. Stanley and Mrs. Betts drove over to the first location and were amazed by what was possible: Castles … towers … rope swings … all kinds of colors and sizes of slides … basketball hoops … ladders … teeter totters … balance beams … wall-ball walls and of course swing sets some so tall that it looked like if the kids really went high enough they would be in the stratosphere. The variety was overwhelming.

The salesman approached them and began his pitch. "So, you are thinking of some equipment for the grandkids and you want to place it in the backyard. I have the perfect idea. We call it the "Game of Thrones Castle." It is set up behind the office. Let me show it to you."

As they walked around to the back of the building they could not believe their eyes. The structure must have been over 10 feet tall and was made of polished wood. All along the top of it were different colored flags flapping in the breeze. It looked more like a middle-ages fort than a toy. It was so massive it would have taken up almost half of the back yard and had every activity imaginable. "For only fifty thousand dollars we will deliver it and set it up for you … for free!" The salesman smiled. "Your grand-kids will love it and play on it all day long. Our researchers have determined that it would take a child over two hours just to try out all the activities possible. And it is on sale!"

Stanley just looked at the salesman and responded, "We didn't pay fifty thousand dollars for our whole house. Forget it."

"Well!" the salesman responded in a sarcastic manner as he walked away. "Thanks for wasting my time. I will go talk to other customers. They probably love their grand-kids more than you two do."

Stanley and Mrs. Betts looked at each other. After a mo-ment Mrs. Betts shouted after the salesman, "We love our grandchildren more than anything in the world. You can't measure the amount of love you have for a child by the number of toys you buy."

Of course, (*sorry for using these words*) the salesman was not about to believe that one.

As Stanley and Mrs. Betts climbed into their pickup truck Stanley offered, "Why don't we try the other company that *Google* mentioned. I have the address and it isn't too far from here."

Mrs. Betts was still upset. "I don't know. I really am not in the mood for shopping right now. Let's go home and see if there is anything on *Craig's List* or *e-bay*."

And there was.

A family living nearby in the Valley was preparing to move to Sun City, Arizona, and had a small three-swing set and metal slide for sale for a very reasonable price. Their children had grown up and the equipment had not been used for some time so it was in need of repair. The buyer would be responsible for disassembling it and removing it from their property. Stanley had no problem with this deal at all and soon he had it loaded in his pickup truck and was on the way home. Mrs. Betts was ready to help repair and repaint and in a couple of days the equipment looked as good as new. "Where do you think we should set it up?" asked Stanley.

"Probably in a shady area so it won't get too hot in the sunshine." suggested Mrs. Betts.

They waited in anticipation for the next time some of the grandchildren would come over. Carter, Aedyn and Maev came by on their bikes for some of Gramma's treats and as they walked out onto the back patio with their hands full they were delighted to see the equipment.

"Last one on the swings is a rotten egg!" shouted Carter as he galloped away.

In minutes all three kids were swinging in total joy. Carter was always kind of a dare devil, so he decided to jump out of the swing a bit higher than one would expect. As he gleefully flew into the air he went a little farther than he planned … right into the koi pond! He let out a loud scream and hit the water with such force that a huge plume rose into the air with a couple of gold fish along with it. He sat there up to his neck in water and in total shock as Maev and Aedyn stopped swinging and ran to help him and put the fish back in the pond. Maev screamed joyfully, "Do that again! That was really cool!"

Of course (again) Stanley and Mrs. Betts heard the ruckus and rushed outside to see what had happened. Carter was okay but soaked like a drowned rat. He didn't appreciate Maev's contribution. Later, Stanley moved the swing set and slide to make sure nobody else got a little goofy.

• • •

The grandkids from Seattle always came over for the 4th of July celebration.

Editor's note: See "Chapter 5 … Born on the 4th of July! Nah" for more information about those festivities.

Stanley decided this would be the perfect time to construct a 'fort' on the living room floor. When the kids were small he would get a couple of kitchen chairs, place a broom and mop handle on the tops of the chairs and drape a blanket over them to make a 'fort.' This time would be entirely different! He sat down at the kitchen table with a large piece of white drawing paper and his pencil and eraser and called the grandkids to join him. Brendan, Connor and Emily stood by and watched in awe as an amazing structure flowed from his mind through his hand and onto the paper. "I have two round card tables and two folding rectangular craft tables that stretch eight feet when they are opened. I will use one of the card tables at one end." He drew a large round circle on the paper. "Then I will open one of the craft tables and put it against the card table." He drew a large rectangle next to the round circle. Then he thought a minute. "I think I will put the second card table against the opened craft table." He drew another large round circle. "Then I will place the next craft table against the card table and finish the design by adding the coffee table."

Emily commented, "It looks like a big bug."

Stanley turned to the kids standing around him and ordered, "Alright you three! Time to go to work! Emily you go around the house and find all the blankets you can. Its summer time so no bed needs two blankets. There are always some stored in the closets. Boys! Start moving the living room furniture to make room for our 'fort.' I will go downstairs and get the tables."

A brief time later Emily walked into the living room with her arms full of blankets. Included was a beautiful patchwork quilt in a clear plastic bag. Stanley noticed that right away. "We can't use that one, honey. That is called a 'quilt' and was made by Gramma's gramma many years ago. It is very precious to her. You should probably put it back where you found it."

Like a well-trained army everyone did their jobs quickly and efficiently. The 'fort' came together like some living creature and in short order commanded most of the living room floor. The assortment of colorful blankets draped over the tables added a glorious touch to their hard work. The kids gleefully climbed under the blankets and into the cool dark interior ready to find places for their sleeping bags. Nobody was going to sleep on any old fashioned beds now that the 'fort' was ready.

As Mrs. Betts walked down the stairs from the office to see how things were going she was startled to see Stanley removing the microwave oven from the kitchen and carrying it toward the 'fort.' "What are you doing?" she asked in a very shocked manner.

"I'm going to put the microwave oven in our 'fort' so we can make some popcorn." Stanley responded.

Mrs. Betts rolled her eyes (probably for the millionth time). "Not on your life! You put that microwave oven back in the kitchen. That's where I draw the line with the 'fort' monkey business."

● ● ●

Every summer Stanley and Mrs. Betts arranged for a day at the nearby theme park. It was one of the best in the country with a huge water park featuring two wave pools and water slides hundreds of feet long, restaurants, a magic show, all sorts of games and rides, a carousel, Ferris wheel, steam engine ride and some of the scariest rollercoasters found anyplace. They had names like "The Toot Squeezer" or "The Tummy Tumbler" or "Into the Jaws of the Demons." The theme park rented cabanas situated on an island between the massive wave pools and Stanley would get one for the day so everyone could enjoy the shade provided and know that their personal effects were safe. Some of the grandkids decided Stanley had arranged for the cabana so he could have a mid-day nap once everyone else was busy enjoying all the activities. The jury is still out on that thought but it may prove to be true.

One particular summer an interesting collection of grandkids were able to join Stanley and Mrs. Betts at the theme park. The two tallest grandsons, Coleman who was 6 feet 6 inches tall and Benny who was 6 feet 5 inches tall arrived along with the two youngest granddaughters. Sofia was 10 years old and Fiona was 4 years old. Once they got settled in the cabana and were able to put on their swim suits Mrs. Betts told the grandkids to pair up and explore around for a while. She gave them twenty dollars in case they wanted to buy some Dippin' Dots or other treat. Big Coleman reached down for Fiona's hand and asked, "What do you want to see?"

Fiona looked up at her giant cousin and responded, "Everything! What did you think?"

And off they went together as people notice the unusual pair. Someone was heard to say, "Well I guess that's the long and short of it."

Benny asked Sofia for her preference. She was always one of the most agreeable ones in the family and answered, "It all looks like fun to me. Let's go where you want to go."

Coleman and Fiona were the more adventurous ones. They headed straight for the roller coasters. It was easy to locate them by just listening for the screaming. Fiona ordered, "I want to go on the "Into the Jaws of the Demons" ride".

Coleman looked down at her in amazement. "Are you sure? It really sounds scary."

The four year old ignored his input, "Come on! Are you a fraidy cat?"

When they got to the line there was a height requirement chart printed on a big wooden board. Anybody too small was not allowed to enter. The ticket taker looked askance at Fiona and said, "Little girl. Go stand by that chart." Well you guessed it. She was quite a bit smaller than allowed.

Fiona was so disappointed she almost started crying. "You are being prejudiced against short people. Coleman and I are going to sue this theme park. And I mean it!"

Her big cousin took her hand and they walked over to the section that had all kinds of rides for little kids. He couldn't believe that a four year old knew all about 'prejudice' and suing people. He was sure she was going to be a politician someday. The park especially liked the little kids so when they found the attractions for the small fries there was plenty to do. Fiona climbed aboard the vintage World One airplane ride and looked back at Coleman. With a big smile she yelled, "Too bad, Coleman, you can't do this ride … you are too tall!" So, Coleman was pretty much an observer while Fiona had a ball. When they came to the Ferris Wheel, thankfully, both could ride together and they had great fun together.

Meanwhile Benny and Sofia wandered around the water park trying to decide what to do first. The selection was amazing. A person would have to visit the theme park more than one day to try everything. Sofia kept eyeing one feature called "Riptide Racer." It was a water slide standing at least 60 feet above the ground with over 400 feet of slide to the pool below. She looked at Benny and said bravely, "Let's try it!"

Participants had to lie on their backs at the top and wait for a bar to raise up before they could begin their adventure. The person operating the starting bar made it very clear that a person must keep straight and flat and be sure to keep his or her hands at their sides. There were four slides attached to each other so up to four people could go at one time. It was his job to be sure the group that went before Benny and Sofia had made it to the pool before he would let them take off. Sofia looked down the 400 or more feet of slide waiting to capture her and began to have second thoughts. There is a big difference between looking up at a giant water slide and looking down.

Just as the bar begin to raise, she yelled, "Nope! Forget it! No way am I going down that way."

Benny turned to look at her and decided that if she wasn't going he wasn't either. He felt responsible for staying close to her. As he pushed up with his arms they slipped on the wet slide and off he went! His head and shoulders were no longer aligned with the slide and it was just enough of an angle to cause him to start going down in a more or less sideways manner. By the time he finished the ride he had tumbled and bounced all the way down and he hit the pool at the bottom with a resounding splash! Two park employees rushed over to help him out and to determine just how seriously he had been hurt. A large crowd gathered around as they carefully removed him from the water and began checking his arms and legs. "I'm okay," he was able to say after he caught his breath.

The employees were not about to take any chances so they ordered a wheel chair and rolled him back to the cabana.

Imagine Stanley and Mrs. Betts' shock when they saw their grandson.

The rest of the day was much more uneventful. Benny was a little shaken up but okay, so he and Sofia ended up having a great time as well as Coleman and Fiona. As the night walked across the theme park all the beautiful lights came on and begin to shine brightly. The entire location looked like the world's biggest Christmas tree. The happy family walked over to ride the Ferris Wheel together so they could see the beautiful site from the top. Many fond memories happened as a result of their time at the park, but one memory Benny was hoping would at some time be forgotten.

CHAPTER 17

"Dudley" the Dinosaur

The autumn months are a time for hard work in Mrs. Betts' backyard. The tree leaves begin to cascade all over the lawn, the needles from the pine trees are blown around by the wind and pile up so thick they look like brown snow drifts. All the annual flowering plants have done their work and their blossoms are dry and colorless so they need to be dug up and disposed of to make room for next year's flowers. Mrs. Betts was gradually replacing the annuals with perennials that bloomed every season so this was becoming less and less an issue for autumn clean-up.

Early one morning Stanley was raking pine needles and fallen leaves and loading them into construction bags to be taken off to the recyclers. In the back corner of the yard where not much grows because the trees block the sunlight, the piles of leaves were ankle deep. His rake slipped over something strange … for anybody's back yard. As he worked the leaves away much to his amazement he noticed something emerging partly from the soil that looked like a plastic light grey soccer ball. He was sure one of the neighbor kids must have kicked it over the fence, so the nice thing to do would be to dig it up and throw it back.

"Hmm," he muttered, "I never played soccer in school, but from what I have seen on TV, I think soccer balls are round. This one kind of looks like a giant jelly bean."

He carefully lifted it from the soil and much to his amazement it looked more like an egg than anything else. "Sweet potato!" he called to Mrs. Betts. "Come and see what I found!"

Mrs. Betts had just put some loaves of her famous homemade bread in the oven when she heard Stanley call out. Still wearing her kitchen apron she hurried through the glass slider to see what he was up to. He looked like a little kid who had just won first place in a pie eating competition. "Well now, what are you holding in your hands. I can't say I have ever seen anything quite like that before." She wondered.

"I think it's a huge egg." Stanley answered. "What do you say we cook it for dinner?"

Mrs. Betts rolled her eyes and responded. "Don't be a silly goose. Who knows how long it has been in the backyard or what kind of bird put it there? If we tried to eat it I wouldn't be surprised if it gave us the worse tummy ache since we tried to eat those clams you found on the beach over by Seattle last summer. Who can forget that?"

Stanley lowered his eyes, "I didn't know clamming season was over and never heard of a 'red tide' before. Nobody ever mentioned that to me. Now that I think about it, I guess they did seem a little more slimy than usual."

After a few moments contemplation, Mrs. Betts conjured up an unusual idea. "What do you say we try to hatch it? If it doesn't work, we are no worse off than before we tried."

So, Mrs. Betts washed the egg in the kitchen sink and Stanley cleared some space on the living room floor, found a small basket, put some comfy blankets in it, placed a table lamp nearby to provide extra heat … and watched it … and watched it … and watched it.

(Editor's note: Here we go with the redundancy again similar to Chapter 5. I guess it does paint a picture.)

Late one night as the two were snuggled down in bed an unpleasant scratching sound echoed down the hallway followed by loud cracking noises. Mrs. Betts and Stanley jumped out of bed and hurried to see what was happening. Much to their amazement in the dim light of the table lamp the egg had changed dramatically. It was no longer smooth. Cracks had formed from one end to the other and already some chunks of egg shell were lying on the floor. As they leaned down to get a closer look they saw big brown eyes peering back at them … And bingo! … The egg fell open and a little green animal crawled out blinking its eyes and making soft sounds like a meowing kitten. You guessed it! It was a baby dinosaur!

Mrs. Betts could hardly speak. "Oh, my gosh! I can't believe my eyes! It's a baby dinosaur! What do we do now?"

Stanley, the more practical person of the couple, answered confidently, "It's probably hungry. I'll go get some peanut butter."

(Editor's note: Your first reaction was probably "peanut butter?" But frankly nobody knows what to feed a baby dinosaur so anything goes.)

The little dinosaur took to the peanut butter like it was the best thing in the world! He was very hungry and went through the jar of "Jif" in nothing flat. As soon as Mrs. Betts removed the egg shells from his bed, he tiredly cuddled down and happily went to sleep. He looked so sweet laying there that Mrs. Betts' heart just opened up. "I think we should keep him. We do need to be sure the cats leave him alone so maybe we should put his basket in our bedroom and keep the door closed. In fact, let's give him a name." She thought a moment and said, "Welcome to the family, Dudley."

Stanley was going to protest, because he knew the truth about taking animals into someone's home: If you name it … it is yours FOREVER!

Dudley proved to be a great pet. He loved to sit on Mrs. Betts' and Stanley's laps and whispered a very pleasant 'purring' sound as he would drift off to sleep. They tried feeding him different kinds of dog and cat food, but he loved peanut butter so it became his main diet. It didn't take long until he was 'house broken' and would do his business in the back yard. There were never any more greenish colored piles on the carpet when the family would get up in the morning. As Dudley grew larger the cats learned quickly to avoid any contact with him which made everyone happier. Mrs. Betts was concerned about how the neighbors would react if they knew she had a dinosaur for a pet. There might even have been some city ordinances against keeping dinosaurs in the city limits so she was careful to let him play outside only after it was dark. Things seemed to be going well … and everyone was happy … until …

Lucky for everyone, Dudley was not a raptor or T-Rex, but it was clear he probably was a brontosaurus and some day would be absolutely HUGE! People who studied dinosaurs say a brontosaurus could grow up to be at least 72 feet long from head to tail … and it was clear it was happening. In a matter of weeks Dudley grew so large on his peanut butter diet that when he sat on Stanley's lap, Stanley groaned in discomfort. "Pumpkin pie!" he called to Mrs. Betts. "Something has got to change."

Dudley would never harm his people on purpose so he didn't understand Stanley's reaction. He wandered off to the master bedroom with hurt feelings; so Mrs. Betts followed him, sat down and gave him some nice peanut butter cookies and some friendly scratches under his neck.

Important family meeting:

Stanley was very distressed. "What are we going to do? He is quickly outgrowing our home. I love him but he is becoming more of a nuisance than a pet. Last night when I let him out to go to the bathroom, he almost couldn't fit out the back slider. I had to buy a small tractor to do the poop scooping and I am running out of places to stack it. When he stretches his neck his head is almost as tall as the roof of our house. One of these evenings Officer Krupke is going to see him and then we will be in deep doo-doo. And I don't mean dinosaur doo-doo."

"I know," Mrs. Betts answered sadly. "I have been worried about that also. I have an idea that I have been putting off because it will mean Dudley will have to leave us; but honestly, I can't think of a better one."

The worse thoughts tumbled through Stanley's mind. "Are you thinking of putting him down? I would never forgive myself if we had to do that. He is probably the last living dinosaur on the planet and needs to be cared for."

Mrs. Betts was upset that Stanley would think of such a thing. "What kind of person do you think I am? A Presbyterian? Dudley is so big and strong I bet some construction company would be very happy to put him to work lifting heavy things and helping to make tall buildings."

And that's exactly what happened!

One of Mrs. Betts' cousins owned Jim Brown Construction Company. After getting over the shock of hearing her story he came to visit and saw Dudley's potential in the construction business. Granted, he was a large green dinosaur, but he was gentle and very strong ... and actually pretty smart, though scientists said dinosaur brains were the size of a pea, so he learned his responsibilities in short order. As long as you kept him in peanut butter he was very content with his new life even though he missed his family at times. Mrs. Betts and Stanley would stop by now and then to check up on him and to make sure he was being treated okay. The construction company built a large barn for him to live in with lots of comfy cushions on the floor and 50 gallon barrels of peanuts butter for him to enjoy. He even had his own 80-inch flat screened TV and loved to watch Fox News.

So, just like in every family, the kids eventually grow up and leave home for new adventures and this was no different for Dudley. His job was to lift large steel beams and hold them in place while the ironworkers welded them to each other. They even let him join United Ironworkers Union Number 704. Since they couldn't sew the identification patch onto his jacket, they made a nice sign and put it in his barn.

If you are interested, you can see him on the job helping build the new Amazon distribution center out west of town. People were parked all along the Interstate Highway watching this amazing event and taking pictures on their cell phones to send to friends and family. The State Patrol had to hang around to be sure people weren't blocking the roadway, so they were less than happy about what was going on. Finally, the Jim Brown Construction Company built a pleasant parking lot for onlookers to park and charged them a dollar each. It became quite the 'in thing' to drive out to the construction site, take a picnic basket and watch. Some people brought peanut butter sandwiches for Dudley and when he was on his lunch break he thought he had died and gone to dinosaur heaven!

… And I am pleased to report that everyone lived happily ever after …

FÜR AUTOREN A HEART FOR AUTHORS À L'ÉCOUTE DES AUTEURS MIA KAPΔIA ΓIA ΣYΓ
OR FORFATTARE UN CORAZÓN POR LOS AUTORES YAZARLARIMIZA GÖNÜL VERELIM S
PER AUTORI ET HJERTE FOR FORFATTERE EEN HART VOOR SCHRIJVERS TEMOS OS AU
SERCE DLA AUTORÓW EIN HERZ FÜR AUTOREN A HEART FOR AUTHORS À L'ÉC
ВСЕЙ ДУШОЙ К АВТОРАМ ETT HJÄRTA FÖR FORFATTARE À LA ESCUCHA DE LOS AUT
ΠΑ ΣΥΓΓΡΑΦΕΙΣ UN CUORE PER AUTORI ET HJERTE FOR FORFATTERE EE
ONKERT SERCE DLA AUTORÓW EIN HERZ F
CÃO ВСЕЙ ДУШОЙ К АВТОРАМ ETT HJÄRTA F

The author

Stan E Hughes, aka Ha-Gue-A-Dees-Sas, (Seneca
for Man Seeking His People), was born on Yakama
Indian country in Washington State and grew
up in the Black Hills of South Dakota. His father
professed being an ah-OH-zee (part-blood) of the
Blackfoot Nation of mid-western North America
and his grandfather carried the blood of the Chica-
ma comico nation of the Chesapeake Bay area.
Hughes is a Vietnam Era veteran and served
from 1959 to 1965. He has earned three college
degrees, is an artist and writer as well as a retired
public school administrator and college supervisor
of student teachers. He was a consultant for
Indian Education Center III at Gonzaga University
in Spokane, Washington, sat on the board of
Spokane's Urban Indian Center, and was active in
Indian Education in Washington and Oregon.
Hughes is the author of several publications
including "Medicine Seeker", "Children of the
Bluefish", and "The Adventures of Sofia - Warrior
Princess."

The publisher

*He who stops
getting better
stops being good.*

This is the motto of novum publishing, and our focus
is on finding new manuscripts, publishing them and
offering long-term support to the authors.
Our publishing house was founded in 1997, and since
then it has become THE expert for new authors and
has won numerous awards.

**Our editorial team will peruse each manuscript
within a few weeks free of charge and without
obligation.**

You will find more information about
novum publishing and our books on the internet:

w w w . n o v u m p u b l i s h i n g . c o m